Seeding Hope

Book 3 in the Possibility Series -

Mending Stone, Catching Rain, Seeding Hope

Sharon Duerst

Praise for Mending Stone

"Mending Stone warmed my heart. It filled my spirit with uplifting whispers of the oft times mystical bond between mother and child, the reality of intuition, and the wisdom of listening to and following your heart." ~*Sue Patton Thoele, author: The Mindful Woman, and The Courage To Be Yourself, among others*

"Excellent. Fabulous. I will read it again! And I want to send a copy to several family members." ~*Kathryn Olmstead*

"I finished Mending Stone in one day! I loved it! I can't wait for the sequel to see what else happens!" ~*Jet McCann*

"I finally read your book, Sharon! You are an amazing writer!" ~*Kim Olmstead*

"A very real account of a woman struggling with grief and self-discovery. Vivid descriptions with true-to-life experiences. The poetry added a thoughtful angle to what was happening. I enjoyed the story within a story. I put the book aside with 36 pages left to read—I didn't want the story to end! A wonderful book! I can't wait for the next one."

~*Simone Neall*

"Very engaging! I really enjoyed it! An adventure!" ~*Bradley Lorang*

"Great job! Can't wait for the sequel! This book brought back great memories of the area I'm from." ~*Connie Van Sickle*

"Reading late into the night, I had to know: why were the two women brought together in such a haunting way? So many questions drew me from page to page to page! The ending was satisfying and sweet—but still I want more!" ~*AnnaMariah Nau*

"It is REALLY good. I couldn't wait to see what was going to happen! It reminds me of a Nicholas Sparks story. And everyone can relate to characters looking to find 'sweetness.'" ~*Judy Bair*

"A gem of a read. It was well written and very descriptive. It reinforced my sense that women should rely on their instincts. I can't wait to read more about Mia and Gerald in the next book." ~*Kay DeBast*

"Sharon...Just finished your book, reading the last 1/3 in one sitting! I thoroughly enjoyed it, and can't wait for more!" ~*Dianne Espy*

"Beautiful. Descriptive. And touching. A perfect read with love, death, mystery, thrills, and humor. A must read for anyone who loves the craft of writing and a spellbinding story." ~*Joseph Duerst*

"You are a talent!" ~*Judy Jacobs Litchfield*

"A spiritual journey pebbled with friends, family, and Native Americans, from the Pacific Northwest to Texas."

~*Ginger Dehlinger, author: Brute Heart*

"I couldn't put the book down!" ~*Kathy Bingham*

"What a lovely read. A very spiritual book, with love crossing the lines of heritage and tradition. The author obviously dug deep into her heart to breathe life into her characters. I've heard there is a follow-up coming soon. Looking forward to it!" ~*Kate Ayers,* author: *A Murder of Crows, A Walk of Snipes, and Eyes & Ears: the Setup*

"Sharon, this is a haunting story that has triggered all manner of questions for me! I paid very little attention to my parents' stories when I was growing up and now they are not available to tell their tales. I found Mia's journey riveting, not just the sleuthing out her Roots, but her reflections on her relationships and development of new ones. What a gifted storyteller you are. Thank you." ~*C. P.*

"Loved your book, read the first 50 pages (in the car) between The Dalles and the Oregon Coast. I can't believe this is your first book! It is so good! I know I will love the sequel, too!" ~*Janet Clark Thomas*

"Hi Sharon, I started your book this weekend and could not put it down and finished quickly. It was really good and you are very talented. Is there a sequel? It would be read! MOVE over Danielle Steel! WOW..."

~*Katrena Meyer*

"I loved it! The story held me to the very end—and then, I cried."
~*Anna Aram*

"Part romance...Scenes with Gerald are full of sexual tension and intrigue; a reader can't help but fall for him...Landscapes are vivid...The mystery unfolds in snippets...Engaging story with developed characters and a sweet satisfying ending!" ~*Gretchen Heberling*

"Enjoyable. Thought provoking. I found myself asking, 'What if...'"

~*Shari Austin*

"Portraits of betrayal, friendship, and loss—with a satisfying outcome of hope." ~*Debbie Wiemeyer*

"I'm reading your book and enjoying it. I have friends standing in line to read it." ~*Mollie Brusseau*

"Nice little touches. Romance is definitely part of it...A slight overlay of fate...Nicely done...Wonderful descriptions..."

~*Rodger Nichols-Haystack Broadcasting*

"Sharon, I read Mending Stone and thought it was beautiful. Your plot was so original and Gerald such a patient, connected person."

~ *Robin Tropzek*

"The descriptive vision brings us directly into the story. I love the interplay of storylines. We're carried with excellent detail into the dramatic story of Rosa, the pace of her hard life. A fun book to read!"

~*Diane Conroy*

"I enjoyed reading this story of a woman learning what it means to have loved and lost, and to travel a path to understanding, healing, and strength. My favorite scene involves her finally claiming her power. And, I loved discovering the answers to the mystery of her family."

~*Maria Carlos*

"I enjoyed Mending Stone. Easy to understand. I also lived in Oregon in that area. Made me feel at home and brought back good memories. Knowing Sharon as a child, I can see her childhood reflected in her stories, and that I mean in a beautiful and positive way. Looking forward to more books, already have Catching Rain. Thank you for pleasure reading. God bless and good luck." ~*Darlene Hohn*

"The woman at the center of this story, Mia Casinelli, is unhappy and doesn't understand why. Maybe it's the lies her life is built on. As her marriage is crumbling, she finds her future opening up. Her disturbing dreams finally begin to lead her on a journey of discovery and enlightenment. She finds new friends, new horizons, new possibilities, along with answers she needs to break free of a past that has kept her bound to misconceptions causing her misery. Mia's journey is tough, but the rewards are great." ~*C. M. Ayers,* author: *A Murder of Crows, A Walk of Snipes, Eyes & Ears: the Setup*

"Haunting. This book cast a spell over me and drew me through Mia's story like a magnet. Hers is a calling that we can relate to, but not many of us have the courage to pursue. Thanks to the author for such a compelling read." ~*Kate Bracy,* author: *That Crazy Little Thing*

"A captivating story—it took me to unknown places that now seem familiar." ~*Karen Martell*

"In Mending Stone, Mia's story is woven together with other women. I wanted to hear their story as much as I wanted to find out how Mia's story would end." ~*Debbie Healy*

"An enthralling read! Well researched, richly descriptive in a unique writing style fitting the story. I wanted to keep reading!"

~*Lisa Anderson,* independent reviewer

Praise for Catching Rain

"Love the story—the mystery unfolding about who Mia is...Love the focus on intuition, and attention to dreams and images...Love the relationships...Love the locations...many of my favorite places...the Northwest...San Francisco...Mexico...What a lovely story! I loved reading this book!" ~Maria Carlos

"I had my coffee and started reading, ate lunch while reading and didn't stop until reaching the beautiful ending! I laughed...I cried...I rejoiced in how Mia changed her life! I loved this story! It reminded me how important it is to take risks in life and move toward what is wanted— even if not knowing at all where it will lead. Following intuition can be life altering! I feel the characters are friends, and I wonder what is next in their lives! I don't want to let them go!" ~Jet McCann

"I loved the depth of the story, and the characters! I couldn't put it down until I finished reading! It was so good! Nothing left out! I loved the ending!! I'm amazed at the places the story went. I want to look up the attractions at the back of the book and plan a Catching Rain Itinerary!" ~Karen Martell

"I could not put this book down! So easy to read...Really flowed. Great story line...Loved reading about the different locations."
~Katrena Meyer

"I truly enjoyed it. I appreciate the characters so much." ~Karen Callin

"A great book! The poetry is fascinating. I love the travel, and especially being able to relate to all the places in the Pacific Northwest. I also love a great love story, and I needed tissue at the end!"

~Connie VanSickle

"This heartwarming follow-up to author, Sharon Duerst's novel, Mending Stone, continues to weave this romantic story of one woman's intuitive connections, leading her to unexpected, yet life affirming results. Sharon Duerst has outdone herself, again." ~*Janet Thomas*

"Catching Rain picks up where Mending Stone left off, tied up loose ends with enough tragedy and heartache, but ends beautifully—exactly where you would want it to!" ~*Debbie Wiemeyer*

"Catching Rain was even more compelling than Mending Stone! I love how the characters developed alone and together." ~*Debbie Healy*

Praise for Seeding Hope

"I so enjoyed the last two books and now this one! Once I got near the end I wanted it to keep going! I love how it ended! What are the possibilities for another book? I will be waiting!" ~*Gloria Bird*

"*Seeding Hope* is about finding oneself after great loss, working through grief and discovering a resilient spirit inside. It tells a lovely story of what can happen after sorrow when one is open to possibilities. For people who read *Mending Stone* and *Catching Rain* this book answers the question "What happened to Mia?" Author Sharon Duerst once again fills her story with poetry through lush descriptions of a Mexican landscape and culture, as well as the Pacific Northwest. She brings the characters to life with well-crafted dialogue and poetic dream sequences...I love this book!" ~*Maria Carlos*

"Having a child changes everything. Walk with Mia and child on the path that is growth on so many levels." ~*Cathy Miller*

"I enjoyed reading *Seeding Hope*. I loved the way you referred to *Mending Stone* and refreshed readers on the past. I felt I was right there with Mia and her family in their joys and sorrows. The end left me wanting the next book on hand to keep reading! I love these novels!" ~*LaDonna Denslinger*

"It made me so happy that Mia had the courage to open her life to new possibilities." ~*Jet McCann*

"Sharon's third book, *Seeding Hope*, may be her best one yet; with her gift for storytelling intricately weaving together people and places, I found it hard to put down." ~*Janet Thomas*

"Following the metamorphosis of Mia has been a true roller coaster ride and *Seeding Hope* does not disappoint…In this third installment, we are treated to Mia's discovery of bliss with her baby and husband settling down to life in Seattle. But, a tragic death leads Mia back to her roots and an examination of herself and what comes next. The highs and lows of everyday existence as viewed through the eyes of this woman are evocative. I loved this book and can't wait for the further adventures."

~*Simone Neall*

"I keep thinking about Mia…who is flawed like all of us. Maybe she sparks in us a hope to finally find what we are looking for. Not another man, child, friend, but peace with God and ultimately ourselves. Therein lies a possibility for an ending of hope…" ~*Debbie Wiemeyer*

"'…rain did more than beat the streets. It beat down her heart.' I liked this a lot!" ~ *Dusty Vonberg*

Seeding Hope ~ Book 3 in the *Possibility Series*

(*Mending Stone, Catching Rain, Seeding Hope*)

This novel is a work of fiction. Names, characters, incidents, and places (except those listed in *Attractions*) are either the product of the author's imagination or are used fictitiously. All characters are fictitious, and any similarity to people living or dead is purely coincidental.

Published by White Spring Publishing

Powell Butte, Oregon

Printed in the United States of America

ISBN: (paperback) 10: 0-9855378-5-X

13: 978-0-9855378-5-2

Library of Congress Control Number:

2016910482

Cover design by Joseph J. Duerst

Back description by Gretchen Heberling

Acknowledgements

Jonathan Duerst, Joseph and Ellen Duerst, Gretchen and Mathew Heberling and their boys, Carsen and Cooper, are my beloved immediate family and helpers! It is a joy to share so much and I am so grateful for every minute we have together!

Our siblings and other family offer great love and help!

Blessings to the first team of readers whose criticisms and suggestions led to many good changes: Gloria Bird, Maria Carlos, Kay DeBast, LaDonna Denslinger, Sandra Fisher, Gretchen Heberling, Karen Martell, Jet McCann, Katrena Meyer, Cathy Miller, AnnaMariah Nau, Simone Neall, Janet Thomas, Connie VanSickle, Dusty Vonberg, Debbie Wiemeyer—thank you for all your insights and interest!

My incredible friends and Facebook friends encourage and inspire me beyond measure!

Much love for getting me out of the house for recreation: Kate Ayers, the Bunko Girls, Kathy Cascade, the Central Oregon Writers Guild, Vicky Dyrdahl, Ingrid Preston, and the great outdoors!

Tremendous thanks to all the readers who generously offer their comments and invaluable perceptions!

Thank you for sharing this adventure with me!

Please help spread beauty, love, and kindness to all!

Enjoy!

Characters Through the Series

Mia Casinelli Maria Isabel Angelina Casinelli Edwards

Tim Edwards Mia's former husband

Valerie Young employee hired to work in the Portland store *Enticements* owned by Tim and Mia

Gerald Native American in Oregon Mia could not forget

Victoria Maria Casinelli Angelo's, "Mother" raised Mia

Angelo Casinelli Husband to Victoria Maria, "Papa" to Mia

Angelina Casinelli Angelo's mother, Mia's "Grandmother"

Joyce Campbell Austin hospital volunteer and friend to Mia who traveled with her to Mexico

Blake Lodger friend at Las Mariposas Hotel in Oaxaca City (In early edition, this character was named Stefan)

Rosa, Rosalia Mysterious woman Mia dreamed as Rosa, but is actually Rosalia, sister to Maria

Manuel, Mano Rosa's husband Mia dreamed was Manuel, but is actually Mano

Guillermo Mano's cousin, first husband (Victoria) Maria

Jaime, Javier Man who rescued Rosa—Mia dreamed was Jaime, but is actually Javier

Places Previously Featured

Portland, Oregon where Mia and Tim lived and owned a business 15 years

Rufus, Oregon small town on Columbia River Gorge where Mia's car broke down

Austin, Texas where Mia was raised

San Antonio, Texas Mia's said birth place

Mexico City also known as *Distrito Federal*, or *D. F.*, capital city of Mexico

Ciudad de Oaxaca, Oaxaca, Mexico where Mia began searching for clues she thought were hidden in words on Victoria and Angelo's marriage license and where she hoped to find similar cloth to a scrap found in an old atlas on a map of Mexico

San Bartolomeo, Italy or Mexico towns Mia searched for on maps in hopes of finding clues about Victoria's past

San Bartolo Coyotepec town in Oaxaca where Mia found unique handcrafted black pottery

San Bartolome Quialana, Oaxaca village Mia and Joyce found on a map, family home of Rosalia

Dedicated to those who keep striving to conquer their fears and their tears and the troubling things of life, and continually look for good

"We are not separate, nor dream alone..."

Looking Back to Mending Stone and Catching Rain

It rained 43 inches in Portland in 2006—seven inches above the previous year which was even higher than the year before. Maybe all that rain precipitated Mia's desire for a child. Maybe it was just time—time to have more of what she wanted. Time to make it happen.

But that year, rain did more than beat the streets. It beat down her heart. Hopes for making a family were dashed in complicated conceptions and heartbreaking miscarriages—the last pregnancy far enough along for her to think she might safely deliver, but then tears poured down like rain and her spirit drowned in another loss.

Though the rain did let up some by the end of spring

2007, Mia still could not shake her dreadful sorrow. By day, she wandered the house—unable to make herself return to the work which had been her only driving ambition for over fifteen years. And her nights were tortured with dreams of devastation: a mysterious woman suffering great loss and longing seeming as real as Mia's own.

Finally, a most disturbing dream of the woman jolted Mia into action to end her devastation and suffering. She formulated a plan to save what was left of her marriage, but was it already too late?

Plans to rekindle romance with husband, Tim, went horribly wrong. Dropping in to surprise him in their Portland, Oregon gift shop, she found him in the arms of Valerie, the young woman hired to "fill in" while Mia was recovering. Leaving the shop in shambles, Mia drove out into the night. Rain, wind, even rocks in the road did not stop her, but a car breakdown did. Hours away from home, high on a ledge above the Columbia River, she teetered with tears in her eyes. She might have tumbled to certain death, but a gust of wind blew her back and strong arms stopped her fall, holding her tight and bringing her down the hillside. Heartbeats pounded in her ears, but her eyes refused to open. She sank down, down into heavy dreams, and woke, bruised and shaking, in a stranger's bed.

Mia could not escape the man offering more than temporary shelter. Gerald's brown eyes held her, warming like coffee he served sweet and white, just how she liked it. And Gerald listened as words fell from her lips, the whole story spilling out as if the coffee was truth serum, as if she could not stop their flow.

Waiting for her car to be repaired, waiting for some sign to go, waiting for an unsettling dread to subside, Mia stayed. By day, anger, guilt, frustration and disappointment tormented her. By night, strange dreams plagued her sleep.

When emotion burned too hot, Mia ran for release on the winding asphalt roads wrapping the rural hills like ribbons. Sun burned her skin, but restless wind pushed her on and on past undulating fields of young wheat.

Words were in her mind: some she did not understand, others she could not bring herself to acknowledge. Dust devils swept over the dry land along the Columbia, but they could not sweep away her sense of failure over so many things.

After years of strained and missed communications with her parents, Victoria and Angelo in Texas, Mia could not tell them of her struggles. She failed to fulfill the most basic tasks of womanhood: making babies and keeping the affection of her husband. And she had lost her faith and all hope in the process.

Where could she now turn for something to shore up her shaky self? What did she need? And where could she find it? Was Gerald offering something she wanted?

The dry air east of the Cascade Mountains, the blue, blue water of the rivers and sky, the wind of the place stirred something in her. Her eyes were open now, noticing everything. And they could not help lingering on Gerald's sun-warmed skin and the dark pony tail hanging down his broad back. When their eyes met, something rose in her— something she could not, would not name. And Mia might have forgotten there was somewhere else she should be, someone else she should be with. But when her car was finished, her commitment and responsibility to Tim nagged at her; she sent a note proposing a meeting at Multnomah Falls, not knowing if he would actually show.

She was not really leaving Gerald's safe haven. Mia was only driving down the Columbia River Gorge to have a necessary discussion. Her hands gripped the wheel. Wind gusted. And maybe Tim wouldn't show and she could go back before the storm hit. But Tim did arrive, and he brought distressing news from her parents: Victoria was terribly ill. Shock and dismay upset Mia's stability. Heated words sounded and Tim tried to end the exchange by forcing her into the car. But then Gerald appeared—inquiring into her safety and pleading for her to stay.

Rain was pouring down. She said she had to go and before she could explain or settle a spate of emotion, he walked away and drove out, her pleas unheard.

Mia was shaken by Victoria's diminishing health and the complacency of Angelo. No one was fighting to keep her alive! And cryptic statements made by Mother further confused and upset Mia. A hospital volunteer, Joyce Campbell, offered friendly distraction, but the strange dreams of the Mexican woman once again plagued Mia.

Grieving her losses, without children, career, husband, or home to return to, where could Mia go? What should she do? She searched for some sign. A chance selection in a writing residency at a retreat in the piney woods of NE Texas marked a way forward. She poured herself into writing the long suffering Mexican woman's story. The manuscript, *Mending Stone*, was submitted for review and likely would be accepted for publication.

After months in isolation, having missed her own birthday and Christmas, Mia returned to Austin to spend time with Angelo only to discover he was in a relationship.

Though she threw herself into activities and work at a book store, growing need in her could not be quelled, a voice in her mind could not be silenced. Something pulled at her, adding to her already shaky sense of identity. Troubling remarks by Victoria nagged her with questions.

An embroidered name, ***Angelita***, on a scrap of cloth, and tattered maps found in an old atlas seemed to point to something—some secret—but what? Needling comments by Grandmother Angelina continued to confuse and confound. Grandmother said heritage was powerful, undeniable. Blood of ancestors was undeniable, but how much did it influence a person? How should they live life? Mia troubled over these questions. And she could not put away lingering thoughts about Gerald—the unforgettable stranger left behind in Oregon.

Mia followed clues to San Antonio. Pieces of Victoria's puzzling past led Mia to Mexico in search of a father and a heritage she hadn't known she was missing. But finding no clear answers, she gave up the search and went with friend Joyce to Puerto Escondido for days of sun and fun.

By the water of an unfamiliar beach, Mia found more than she could have been imagined, more than she might ever before have believed possible: the mysterious woman she dreamed—Rosalia—was waiting for her in a shop named ***Angelita***.

Information and explanations of why Mia had been

separated from her mother were complicated by Rosalia's sudden and severe health problems. Once again, Mia kept vigil at a mother's bedside, praying for time—time for finding answers and making amends. But would her prayers be heard? Would *La Virgen* listen now? Did she ever?

Mia's newly renewed faith was tested. How could she move forward? What did she want? And where did she want to be?

Dr. Lanzo Grimaldi, Rosalia's physician, prescribed a restorative journey. A visit to Rosalia's ancestral home revealed surprises and opportunities posing challenging choices for Mia. Could she unlock the mysteries of her life, let go of grief and longing? Did Lanzo hold a key?

Joyce said Mia must let herself *feel*, but already she felt too much! Facing financial woes, Mia made tough decisions that could change more than a few lives. But did she have enough courage to see them through?

Water glistened like hope in Seattle. Mia began a new life, but it was not long before awareness of a strange heaviness forced her to see a new path. Each step moved her closer to the life she wanted and prayed for. But returning loneliness threatened to derail her resolve. A 'chance' meeting with Gerald led to surprising fulfillment of her fondest hopes and desires.

Wind

Mia stirred in her sleep.

Gerald reached for her, his thick hand gentling down from shoulder to hip.

Mostly asleep, she snuggled into the space between his arm and chest. A ragged breath rose from her.

Time! Change come. Wake up!

Her eyes opened. "Ger..." she whispered.

"Hmmm?"

She raised up on an elbow, eyes glancing over to the baby sleeping on a blanket beside them on the hard packed dirt floor. She relaxed down, and sighed. "I dreamed—I don't know *what* now, but it was upsetting."

"Just a dream," Gerald mumbled.

"After all that's happened, you say it's just a dream? After all the hints and signs leading us to find each other—not once, but twice? After all we've been through, you say, 'Just a dream?' Don't you believe dreams lead us somewhere, tell us things important?"

His head turned, dark brown eyes resting on her tense face. "I only mean don't fret. Things have a way of working out."

She sighed. "Our wedding celebration here was perfect with everyone coming! It was the event of a lifetime, sweetness to savor for years and years. And I love being with my new family. But I'm ready to go to *our* home, ready for you to start back teaching, ready for autumn and rain, and even ready for Peyton to crawl!"

Gerald smiled, removed his arm from beneath her head, sat up, and sighed, "Time."

Her head turned, her eyes staring at him. "Time?"

"For coffee," he replied getting up. He pulled on his pants and a t-shirt. "I'll go get some."

Mia rested on an elbow and studied Peyton sleeping. Weeks playing in the Mexican sun had darkened his already warm-toned skin. "Ohhh, baby. We're all family, a great big multicultural family," Mia whispered. "More family than I ever dreamed I could have: no first or second cousins, but other cousins and aunts and uncles and even a great-great grandmother! What a miracle to find them!"

A dog barked somewhere outside. Voices sounded.

The weathered door of the room opened and Gerald came through carrying two mugs. "Last morning here," he said handing her a coffee.

She nodded, then gulped down the sweetened white cup of brew. "Thank you. Just how I like it! You're so good to me!"

"Try to be. Y' give so much. Have to keep up with my beautiful wife," he said easily with a grin.

"My handsome husband. Married in two countries and I still can't believe this dream come true," she breathed. "We're so lucky! Would you mind if I go for a quick walk? Will you stay with Peyton?"

He shook his head, his eyes on her as she pulled back her dark hair in a quick braid. "Good for y'," he smiled. "We'll be fine here," he replied, settling down on the bed.

Mia slipped on a cotton dress and sandals, then came over, leaned down, and planted a kiss on his lips.

Gerald held her arm.

She kissed him again.

"Tell her hello," he said with a sly grin.

"How'd you know?"

"I know what y' want," he answered warmly. "Still hoping for more answers and clarity?"

"I am," she whispered.

"Y' won't find 'em outside," he gently tapped her chest with his fingers. "Here is what y' need."

She blinked back tears. "Probably."

He took a sip of coffee, and got up, saying quietly, "I'll start packing."

"That'd be wonderful."

He smiled, reached for her again.

They kissed, bodies pressed close.

But she pulled away, and went out the door and across the courtyard. Mia slipped through the wooden gate and hurried along the dusty path.

The ancient *Ahuehuete* stood amidst blades of grass feathering the ground. Mia sat down, stretched out, and looked up through the tree's branches. "You're a wise old mother tree, aren't you? So many human lifetimes in your tree-time. Have you had many companion trees? You stand alone here. Did you let many others go?"

Leaves of *Ahuehuete* fluttered.

"A connection led me to Mexico. I found my real mother. But it is her life here, not mine. I have a start in Seattle with Gerald. Did you know when I visited here before what was to come? Did you know about my baby, Peyton? Did you help deliver him to me?" She blinked back tears and glanced up. "Thank you," she whispered. "Thank you for helping. We're leaving today, please take care of the family while we're away. Will all be well?"

Leaves stilled.

Mia rubbed chill bumps from her arms.

Village sounds filled her ears: clatter of household chores beginning and laughter drifted through the air.

Mia hurried back up the trail, reached the entrance gate of the family compound, and pushed the heavy wood door open just as a young man was exiting. "*Primo!* (Cousin!) Off to work so early? You're so hard working!"

Otilio nodded and grinned.

"I'm sorry I won't see you later."

"Someday I come Seattle! City have much work?"

"Yes, there's work. But you need an education."

"Maybe Gerald teach me!"

"He teaches young children. If you come, we can help you there. But you must come legally," Mia warned.

"No *coyotes*!"

Otilio blanched.

"Those immigrant smugglers take your money and don't keep you safe!"

"I work, save money! Maybe one year I come."

"Good to be flexible, allow for unexpected changes and complications..." she said, but her brow furrowed as if unsure why she it. Well, good luck! You'd better be off to work," Mia said giving a quick hug and smile. "Good-bye for now."

He smiled and waved, then went out the gate of the family compound and down the lane.

Family members in the main house were preparing food and setting the table when Mia came inside. She greeted and hugged each of them.

On Gerald's lap and grinning with a mouthful of food, Peyton looked over and babbled at her.

"Oh, baby!" she giggled, kissing his hair. She kissed her husband's head, too. "Thank you for getting him up."

Gerald nodded while assisting Peyton with a drink.

Rosalia, Mia's mother, came from the kitchen with a bowl of peeled and sliced fruits. "Where you go?"

"*Ahuehuete*. I wanted to have a talk before leaving."

Rosalia paused, "*Ahuehuete* answer?"

Hands around the room stilled. Heads turned and eyes darted from woman to women around the room.

"Sometimes I *do* think she responds: leaves flutter with no apparent wind. And then they still suddenly."

Heads nodded, but attention shifted away when Peyton began fussing loudly to get down and play with cousins.

After finished with their packing, Mia left Gerald and Peyton napping while she went over to see Marisol and Benito, the children she'd unofficially fostered. Their aunt's home was as unkempt outside as it had been when Mia visited the year before, but Mia's eyes filled with tears as Benito came running.

"Mama Mia!" he cried and clung to her leg.

She laughed as they squeezed through the door to the house. Elodia greeted her, and Mia sat down. Marisol came from the kitchen and huddled at Mia's feet with Benito. Mia's eyes took in new fabric covering Elodia's easy chair, and flowers in a glass on the table brightening the otherwise faded décor. With Marisol translating, she addressed Elodia, "I pray your health has improved."

"Thanks to all goodness. Marisol is a blessing to our needs. And money sent helps."

Mia inquired about each of the children. And then

she asked about school. Marisol's face clouded.

"What?" Elodia demanded to know.

In a meek voice, Marisol asked, "*Como hacer en la escuela?* (How do I do in school?)"

"Much time needed caring for house and cousins and Benito," Elodia answered in Spanish.

"Marisol needs an education," Mia stated with obvious concern showing on her face. "Are there separate grades, enough classrooms and sufficient teachers for San Bartolome Quialana's children?"

No one answered.

Mia's eyes narrowed. "I'm sorry, Elodia. I send money to meet Marisol and Benito's physical needs, but also their social and educational needs."

Elodia's smile tightened.

Shifting her focus, Mia said affably, "Benito looks good. His facial scars have healed and his smile is beautiful! Now he appears his age! He looks as if he's grown inches and inches and has muscles in his arms and legs that were so skinny before!"

The four year old grinned, his dark eyes gleaming up at her.

Mia's hand brushed over Benito's hair. "Marisol and Benito were like my own children the months they were with me in Seattle. I've missed them so much. I want only the best for them."

Marisol smiled, and Benito put a hand to his mouth, hiding his shy grin.

Elodia commanded her own three children lingering behind her chair to go outside with Marisol and Benito. Then she said plainly, "*My* family! Not you!"

"You're doing a good job. I see your efforts, Elodia. But Marisol is smart. She can learn much and be more help to the family with education. Please let her go to school."

Elodia seemed to understand, but made no comment except for a sharp glance and slight lowering of her chin.

Parting words were spoken.

Mia departed after tearful good-byes.

It was late morning when the car wound through the streets. Rosalia, Mia, and Peyton in the back seat glanced out the windows at villagers waving.

"Sweet friends here!" Rosalia's light brown eyes gleamed and exchanged glances with her husband, Javier, in the front seat beside Gerald.

"Our wedding together was so special!" Mia sighed.

"Dream come true!"

"It was perfect! Wasn't it husbands?" Mia leaned

forward and patted the men's shoulders.

Javier nodded, smiling and wiping tears from his dark brown eyes. "Wife beautiful! *Hermosa!* Big party! Much music and fun with family and village friends!"

Gerald's eyes caught Mia's in the rear-view mirror and they smiled at each other.

"Even Joyce, Papa and Maggie, and Grandmother Angelina!" Mia shook her head, "Ger, it was such a sweet surprise! I don't know how you kept the secret! I thought you tell me everything..."

His eyes held her but Gerald's smile faded.

The village was left behind. The valley stretched out ahead like a peaceful promise.

Nearly two hours and many minutes of entertaining the baby later, the car was climbing a rough, winding road.

"Ugh! I remember this! Last time, I thought the curves and swerves made me queasy, but being pregnant probably was responsible. I should've guessed that."

"I know!" Rosalia said with a grin.

"You did? Why didn't you tell me?"

"Not for mother say. For daughter to know first."

"Was a long time until y' knew," Gerald said catching her eye again. "Guess y' were busy with Marisol, and Benito's surgery, and getting settled in Seattle. Ended well, though."

Mia sighed, glancing over at Peyton. "Probably better I didn't know. I would have been so anxious after losing so many before." Brow knitted in concern, Mia looked out the window as if watching for dangers. "I don't ever want to suffer like that again! Losing the babies, then my marriage, career, Mother. Too much heartbreaking loss."

Gerald watched her in the rear-view mirror. "Y' can handle whatever comes y'r way. Y' have strength now."

"You're my strength," she replied.

Rosalia shook her head. "Is life! Sometime hard. Have baby, good man! Give thanks!"

Grinning, Javier nodded.

"My life *is* so good. And I *am* thankful now for all the turns taken, the unexpected answers to prayers."

"Daughter have faith?"

"Yes, but my mind slips back into worry at times. I need to keep trusting."

"*Madre* answer need!" Rosalia said exasperated.

"There are so many things I *want* to make happen! And I want to put struggle behind."

Rosalia only shrugged. "Life—joy and struggle."

Gerald was pulling the car into a parking lot. He and Javier got out, and opened the back doors for them.

"Hierve el Aqua!" Mia exclaimed, handing Peyton out to Gerald.

"We see 'Water Boils'?" Javier asked.

"Not really. Streams of spring water—calcium carbonate and other minerals—dribble over the edge and down the hillside, leaving formations looking like waterfalls."

They walked toward small natural pools and several artificial pools constructed for swimming close to the edge of the cliffs.

"Look like infinity pools," Gerald remarked.

As they neared the precipice, Javier stopped and sat down where he was. But Rosalia boldly marched forward, removed her sandals, and waded in, exclaiming, "AHHH!!"

Gerald waded in up to his knees and hung Peyton down, dipping his little feet in the water, then pulling him up giggling. Mia watched and smiled, her eyes gleaming. But her face sobered as if alerted to some danger when words came to her mind.

Tears

fall

This too

is life

She walked over to the edge of the pool and looked down to the valley covered in green grass.

"Go see?" Rosalia asked.

"I'd love for Gerald to see it."

Rosalia watched her husband sitting awkwardly far back from the edge. "Javier stay safe! Wait with him."

Mia nodded, and took Peyton from Gerald. "Mama, can little one stay with you?"

"We watch," Rosalia answered as Peyton leaned toward her waiting arms.

Mia and Gerald walked to the edge of the steep hillside, made their way down a trail to a vantage point of the sea-foam green plummeting toward the valley.

"Isn't it amazing? Only a little mineral water dribbling over the edge and building up makes the illusion of falls. I guess we never know what can develop over time."

"Pretty." Gerald reached out a hand to her.

As she clasped it, words flooded into her mind.

Body and soul

Reach across expanse

Like endless roots

Gerald smiled a lover/husband's smile.

"So much has happened since I came here last year with Mama." Mia turned to look again at the "foamy" mineral deposits. "The hazy colors remind me of your paintings. Ethereal and suggestive of somewhere in time."

"Interesting."

She sighed, looking up at the trail. "Going back will be hard."

"More adventures together through ups and downs."

"More like downs first, then ups," she said with a laugh. "Hopefully, no more downs!"

Starting on the trail, she said, "Ugh! I'm fat and out of shape! I need to get fit like I did running. But two years ago, sadness and anger pushed me onward. It was needed therapy! I've been much too satisfied this year to get motivated!" Mia paused for a rest. "I gained happiness and pounds."

"Bit of gain myself," Gerald agreed, breathing hard.

"You look fine," she sighed with a warm smile.

"Feel heavy. Maybe elevation," he said pounding his chest for emphasis. "Maybe just elevation."

She nodded, and they saved their breath while climbing silently up the steep hillside.

Water

The flight to Puerto Escondido from Oaxaca City was several hours shorter than the eight hours it would have taken to drive over the mountain pass to the coast.

"Too much money for this!" Rosalia objected.

"Worth it, Mama! The van we took last time was in bad repair but the road is too curvy and full of potholes and hazards for any vehicle. And with the baby…"

Rosalia shrugged. "Is Mexico."

"Some advantages we get to enjoy now! Besides, our husbands love flying!" They turned to see Javier grinning and staring out the window, Gerald dozing.

"We can relax. Nothing else we must do," Mia whispered over the head of her baby sleeping on her chest. "Isn't he the sweetest?" His plump little hand gripped her side. "I put off getting pregnant at least ten years because I thought a baby would add to already endless chores and drain my love and care. I thought mothers give and give and give with little returned love until years later. I didn't know babies, even this small, can love back!"

"*Ay,*" Rosalia sighed. "This I remember: weight of baby, smell of sweet hair." She shook her head. "Many time over years, I think of this and my heart go to you. I pray, hope, dream someday I see again!" Tears glistened in her eyes. "More than forty years I dream…"

Mia patted her mother's hand. "I can't imagine your suffering and loss, how you got through it! Terrible you could not return to your parents, beyond horrible what happened! Husbands should take care of wives, not…" but Mia paused and could not continue.

"*AY…*" Rosalia sighed, but did not have an episode as with other times when talking of the time long ago. "My heart hurt. So much I cry! But sister say no cry! Maria make plan. But something go wrong. I pray safe. Somewhere think find. But nowhere. *Ay,* how heart hurt! No answer for prayers! Only years waiting, no sister, no daughter come.

But have Mano. Then also Mano go and no return. Heart break again. *Ay!* Cry so much! And anger grow like beast!"

Mia watched her mother closely, "I don't see anger in you now."

Rosalia stole a look back at her husband. "Heart break. Evil words fall from mouth and Devil listen! Pray forgiveness, but cry and wish again Mano burn in passion! Evil wish come for me! I pray *Dios* take me. But *Dios* no listen. Even *Madre* no listen to sinner. *La Virgen* good. *She* suffer. *Madre* lose child. But *She* no wish evil on husband."

Rosalia was shaking her head, but light flashed in her eyes. "Maybe *La Virgen* listen to heart, not words! Javier find in road. Herbs and care heal more than body. Heart broken, black like stone. No hope mending stone. But Javier talk. Talk, talk, talk, say so much! Words like magic reach me. Tears fall from eyes like rain, make heart of stone soft again." Rosalia rubbed her arms and face. "Fire and sun burn, but new skin grow. *I* grow."

"Just like I dreamed, and wrote in *Mending Stone*! Isn't it strange how I somehow knew your story and wrote it long before I ever found you? I must have dreamed the images for words I couldn't understand since I barely speak any Spanish and you didn't speak much English back then. Somehow, I *heard* the story, saw it in my mind."

"Emotion speak."

"I think you're right! Hearts understand. I longed for someone, something I didn't have. And I dreamed of a woman. I understood her pain, heard her pleas, shared her lament. I knew her devastation of losing a child; it was like my own. But I had no idea what I wrote was *literally* the story of my life and yours!"

Rosalia smiled, nodding.

Stirring on Mia's chest, Peyton opened his eyes, turned his head, and re-settled.

"Love stretches over miles like endless roots reaching for nourishment," Mia said. But other words came suddenly to her mind.

Wind scatter hopes

Water wash away dreams

Seeds of plans whisk away

on silent beating wings

After arriving in Puerto Escondido, they went to Rosalia and Javier's house. On the patio at the edge of the bluff above Playa Carrizalillo, Mia stood watching the tide.

"Welcome back!" boomed a man approaching.

"Oh, hello," she breathed, seeing the doctor.

"I'm here for a favorite patient," Lanzo Grimaldi said with warm smile.

"So kind of you to make a house call for Mama."

"I heard *you* would be here."

"We were in San Bartolome Quialana before this," she stammered.

Watching her push back a lock of hair blowing in the breeze, he said quietly, "We have catching up to do."

Mia's hands gripped the waist-high wall of stucco at the edge of the patio. "Lanzo, I…"

But his hand patted hers before she could finish. "Not to worry. Rosalia has kept me well posted on your welfare since you left last year."

"Ohhh, good." Mia sighed. "I didn't know. So you are aware I…married, have a child?"

He nodded, "But something I need to know…"

Her eyes searched his face, noticing the silver in his hair, the dark brown eyes staring back at her with interest.

"Is he healthy?"

"The baby? Yes," she replied, releasing a breath. "I was shocked and worried when I discovered I was pregnant: so far along and with no prenatal care after so many miscarriages and losing one baby closer to full term two years before. But it seems someone was watching over us."

"Thank goodness. You might have discovered your condition sooner if you'd taken my advice for a checkup when Rosalia was hospitalized. Likely some of the distress you were experiencing then was due to the pregnancy."

"Yes," she sighed. "But it has all turned out well."

Lanzo's eyes rested on her face.

"Dr. Grimaldi," Rosalia said coming out the glass door of the house. "Good to see my favorite doctor!"

"Good to see you," he responded. "Javier at home?"

"Working. Return later. Come back evening? We make special dinner!"

Dr. Grimaldi smiled, but looked over to Mia.

"Yes, come back if you can," she answered.

"Thank you. I believe I will."

"Good!" Rosalia chimed. "Now talk of health."

Mia watched them go inside before she went over to the detached bedroom/bathroom Javier had built for her near the main house. She peeked inside. Gerald was propped up on the bed with Peyton snuggled into the crook of his arm. They were both sleeping. She returned to the main house.

Dr. Grimaldi was taking Rosalia's pulse. "Each visit to your homeland seems to improve your condition!"

Rosalia nodded. "Heart heal at home."

"Perhaps influence of the milder temperatures."

Overhearing, Mia interjected, "Likely love of family and friends make the difference. Grandmother, especially."

"Your grandmother is still living, Mia?"

"*My* grandmother!" Rosalia grinned.

"Women of your family are long living it seems," Dr. Grimaldi commented.

"Not all. But Grandmother have special strength. Some give to me!"

Dr. Grimaldi chuckled, his brown eyes assessing Rosalia's demeanor. "The visits seem to enliven you."

"Good there," Rosalia replied quietly.

"Seems you feel a new, stronger sense of purpose," Lanzo suggested while he watched as Mia began tidying the kitchen.

Rosalia nodded. "Work good for make life easier. Not only for us, but for big family."

"How are Mia's little charges, Marisol and Benito? Have they adjusted back home with their aunt?"

"Benito is healing well from the cleft lip and palette surgeries. Marisol is a bright seven year old, but she doesn't seem to be in school. I think her aunt, Elodia, keeps her busy with constant household duties. I am only just learning the culture of Mexico, and Oaxaca, but I have a hard time accepting interrupted education. Girls and young women need learning! They are caretakers of the next generation, educators of their families! And so many of them nowadays are left to fend for the family when the men leave the community to seek employment in the cities in Mexico and the United States. San Bartolome Quialana has a huge percentage of citizens leaving, most of them men."

Rosalia shrugged. "True now, true before."

"It's frustrating! I have great hopes for Marisol and Benito. I thought I could make a real difference in their lives. I brought them to Seattle for Benito's surgeries and Marisol making friends in America to practice her English. I wanted to broaden more their views of the world!"

"No doubt you've altered their lives through your intervention and caring," Lanzo offered. "It's a difficult life for orphans, especially living in isolated villages with limited chance for economic growth or prosperity."

"Marisol should be learning to take advantage of many different kinds of opportunities, not being a slave to her aunt!" Mia replied in agitation.

"Not Mia's children! For aunt to say," Rosalia scolded. "Mexico, not U.S."

Lanzo chuckled, "I'm sure we've not heard the last of this. However, I must be getting to the hospital to check on other patients. My day off, but care is always needed."

"A good man, and a good doctor," Mia replied with warmth.

He smiled at them both. "Thank you. And thanks for the dinner invitation, Rosalia; I'll be happy to return later. Tell Javier, the match is on!"

Rosalia laughed and nodded.

"I'll let myself out! See you both later," the doctor said with a wave as he went out the door.

Mia turned to her mother, "What was that all about? Lanzo seems very friendly and familiar with you now."

"Come often. Teach Bridge. Fun! Maybe you play. And Gerald! More people, more fun! Hard learn first, but get easy."

Mia laughed, "Mama, you are amazing!"

"No want get old! Fight with this!" she replied, pointing to her head and smiling. "Keep try something new; this learn from daughter."

"You're not old! Not even sixty yet! No grey hair and your skin is so young looking!"

"Magic herbs Javier use take years from face!"

"I could use some of those! But, Mama, what did you learn from me?"

"Daughter say strong woman try many things.

Work good, but not good do only this. Mind, body, spirit need change for making good health."

"Meeting Gerald marked a change in me and a new start. It seemed my beliefs transformed as I wrote *your* story of faith, perseverance, and determination."

"What determination?"

"You weathered hard years waiting for your sister to return, for me, and also your husband, Mano. You kept hope alive. I don't know how you did that! You sewed and established yourself as an excellent seamstress. You showed indomitable spirit and a nose for business."

Rosalia shrugged, smiling. "Nose say now make supper for company!"

"We won't need to make much extra with only one guest coming."

"Two."

"Is Javier bringing someone home?"

"Doctor bring friend."

"Oh," Mia paused. "I didn't hear that."

"Always bring Lady, from Texas."

"A woman friend?"

"'Lady' play Bridge."

"Oh. I guess it'll be no more awkward for me around her than for him with Gerald."

Rosalia stared. "Daughter and doctor?"

"We saw each other a few times when I was here last year. It wouldn't have worked out though, even if I had stayed. But he was very kind, and at the time, I needed someone to shore me up."

"Who'd y' need?" Gerald asked, entering the house with Peyton in his arms.

"My big and little men!" Mia squealed. "Look at you both all flushed from your naps!"

"Just resting my eyes," Gerald objected, a hint of a smile on his full lips. "Didn't want to disturb the boy."

"Of course!" she replied, kissing him and holding out her arms to Peyton.

"Mind if I grab a little fresh air?"

Mia shook her head, accepting Gerald's kiss, and watched as he walked away and broad shoulders easing through the doorway. She exhaled a long breath.

"Okay?"

"Silly worry. He seems…I don't know. Different."

Rosalia shrugged. "Men different every day!"

Peyton was squirming. Mia set him down, and he crawled around while they worked on the meal.

"I don't know Bridge. Is it gambling?"

Rosalia laughed. "Not so much. But fun!"

"How did you get started doing it?"

"Doctor say good for mind. Javier like Doctor. Like smart friend and hobby. Many years husband travel many miles from mountains to city, sell things, meet people. But here, with house in town, Javier restless. Husband Gerald restless?"

Mia's brow furrowed. "Men do love to wander outdoors don't they? It almost *kills* them settling in cities."

"Men need *something!*" Rosalia chuckled. "Gerald like house in Seattle?"

"Seems so. He'll be glad when he starts back at school next week. Teaching gives him variety, and making art again will be good. Artists must create, or die."

Rosalia nodded. "Javier artist—make things with hands. Doctor say Javier good health!"

"You're both well and busy creating," Mia said glancing around the room at the colorful cushions Rosalia had sewn for the seating area and drapes for the big windows. Her eyes looked out to the patio and beyond to the wide sky. "So beautiful this house you made at the beach."

Rosalia sighed, "Good thing daughter like beach! Maybe never come over mountains from Oaxaca valley! Beach say something to me when come with Javier. Whisper stay. Whisper heart need here. Now sometimes San Bartolome Quialana say something to me."

"It must have been hard being away from your home and family more than forty years."

"Especially *Abuelita* Inez."

"My life is blessed with Gerald and Peyton and family, and the friends I've made. But lately something pulls at me..." she paused and hurried over to the window where Peyton was fussing behind the generous curtains.

Rosalia smiled, her eyes resting on Mia helping him find a new spot to play with a wooden spoon and a pot.

"Making good music, son!" Mia laughed as Peyton pounded. "You have an ear!"

"One ear? *Bebe* (baby) have two ears!"

"Yes, two ears, but the phrase, 'have an ear' is a reference to natural musical talent: being able to replicate beats and make melodies without instruction."

"Ahhh, daughter good teacher."

"I do believe in life-long learning," Mia responded. "That's why I'm so concerned about Marisol's education."

"Mexico," Rosalia shrugged. "City girls do sport, learn career. Even dress modern. But country girls work house, make craft, sell something. Same when young or old. Not much change in years."

"But things can change, even in the villages. I want

Marisol to have more opportunities."

"No say what Marisol do!"

"We're all connected. We're not only here for ourselves, are we? We need to care about our place and our role in the broader world. I want Marisol to use her passion for painting and also what speaks to her mind and other abilities. I want her to learn sooner than I did how to exercise all kinds of talents! School can teach her..."

"Mother teach *son!*" Rosalia interjected, pointing to alert Mia's attention to Peyton trying to pull up on the couch and dangerously close to toppling over onto hard tile.

Mia retrieved him, and set out some bowls and more implements for him to play with. "Sending money to Elodia is not doing enough for the children."

Rosalia shook her head. "Money can't fix all! Life good! Just live!"

"Perhaps upbringing and circumstances play a part in development, but education *is* important to make a new world with smart people to conquer complex problems."

"Conquer problem there!" Rosalia pointed at Peyton nearing the staircase.

"Little man, little man," Mia said scooping up her boy and kissing his round cheeks as he giggled and squirmed in her arms.

"Maybe a snack will settle you down!" She fixed a bottle, and went with him out to their room. Pushing the door open, Mia glanced inside. "I thought you went for a walk…"

But Gerald failed to reply.

She went around the bed, saw he was sleeping, and settled down beside him to feed Peyton the bottle.

Gerald's breathing and the waves lapping the shore on the bay below filled her ears. She closed her eyes.

Seeds like hope beneath cold ground
warmed by sun, sprout beginnings
push back darkness
with new life

Animals

Mia watched as Lanzo came in with his friend.

"Pleasure to meet, you," Lady said sweetly as if she were a demure young woman, not a skinny, well-endowed middle-aged woman with teased blond hair and a heavy coating of makeup.

"And you," Mia replied nicely, and introduced her to Gerald. He and Javier chatted with the guests while she and Rosalia finished last preparations for supper

Lanzo and Lady, Gerald and Mia sat on either side of the large table of thick old wooden planks. Javier and Rosalia served seafood ceviche with grilled tuna, avocado, peppers, and tomato with cilantro and lime.

"How delightful," Lady commented. "So colorful and fresh tasting! And what a lovely table."

"Husband make this," Rosalia exclaimed with pride.

"You're a wonder, Javier!" Mia said. "We're lucky Mama found you!"

"Javier save old thing in road!" Rosalia exclaimed with bright smile. "Burned, broken. Animals might eat! But Javier find, heal with herbs and sing."

"Singing, too? I haven't heard this part."

Javier grinned.

"True! Javier talk, talk talk. Sing! Man push and push, 'Say something. Say something. Make something beautiful for table.' Javier buy needle, thread, cloth, even thimble! At first, stitch and say nothing, feel nothing. But every stitch heal. Then words come. First angry. Then thankful. Have love. Hope."

"And now woman no quiet!" Javier laughed.

Rosalia playfully patted him while they returned serving dishes to the kitchen.

"Makes a good story," Gerald commented.

"I'd like to hear more!" Lady said.

"Yes, it's fascinating."

"Eat!" Rosalia commanded.

"Please tell the whole story about how we all met: you and me and Javier. Please?" Mia begged.

"No, no. Read story daughter write!"

"You're a writer, Mia?" inquired Lady. "I had no idea we were in the company of greatness."

Laughing despite her shy reserve, Mia answered, "Greatness? No! My debut novel is coming out. I'm calling it an untraditional romantic mystery. Strangely, I dreamed much of it. Other parts were as if someone told me the story. Words were in my mind and emotion as real as my own filled my heart." Her gleaming eyes met Rosalia's. "Turns out, the questions I had and clues I followed led me to Puerto Escondido, and finding the mother I did not know I had lost."

"I'm captivated!" Lady exclaimed with hands clasping together in prayer-like gesture. "Your writing sounds fascinating. The story must be quite extraordinary!"

Mia blushed. "Thank you. That is very sweet of you to say. I hope people like it."

Rosalia fetched another dish—*ensalada de arroz*—corn with diced avocado, tomato, zucchini, peppers, and rice salad. A special portion minus the onions and peppers was made for Peyton. He pushed handfuls of it into his mouth, and grinned.

Next served were *tlayudas*—large flour tortillas, called *blandas*, topped with *frijols* (refried beans), *tinga* (shredded chicken), and peppers, tomato, avocado, and *queso* (cheese) Another *tlayuda* was constructed with no chicken, but did have a generous amount of mushrooms.

"Oooo, Mama! I love the vegetarian one! This is so delicious! Like mushroom pizza! Almost," she grinned. "I still favor bread dough and pasta over tortillas, but they're growing on me. This is nicely grilled, so it's crunchy and more like a thin pizza crust."

"*Frijoles* in place of tomato sauce. Very good!" Gerald added with appreciative smile.

"Rosalia tells us you're a teacher," Lanzo ventured.

Chewing, Gerald nodded. "Art integrated through-out the curriculum. A forward thinking elementary school."

"I'm quite a patron of the arts. What medium do you prefer?" Lady asked, oozing polite interest.

"A draw between photography and painting."

"Might I have seen your work on exhibit?"

"Couple of Northwest galleries have some pieces. But too busy this year to put out anything new. Definitely on the list for the future."

Lady nodded, and smiled, and they all continued to eat. Animated conversations around the table were interspersed with interludes of baby noise.

Dessert was fresh berries in yogurt topped with curls of chocolate.

Lanzo patted his abdomen. "Rosalia, dear woman, and Javier, you have rendered me incapable of Bridge playing tonight! I am too well satisfied to throw my fortunes to the whim of the cards."

"Oh," Mia whined, "I was hoping you could teach us to play!" But then she added, "Actually, I'm also too full for comfortable sitting or concentrating!"

"A beach walk would assist digestion."

"I'm sure it would!" she smiled. "Maybe after we put Peyton to sleep."

"Go, go! *Bebe* sleep in many arms of *Abuelas* (Grandmothers) Rosalia and Lady."

"Don't forget old *Tio Lanzo* (Uncle Lanzo)! I can take a turn if he fusses."

"And me!" Javier offered. "Arms ready!"

They all laughed at his comical expression and gestures for holding a large toddler.

"Many ready and capable arms! We would love a few minutes on the beach," Mia replied with a questioning look to Gerald.

He nodded. "Tomorrow—fourteen or more hours on

the plane with Peyton—could possibly be trying; a walk now would be great. Thank you!"

Mia and Gerald soon went out the door, across the patio, and down the path to the beach.

She scuffed her feet in the squeaky, dry sand. Her eyes looked up to the sky and she pointed at a cloud layer hanging above. "White like *semifreddo*, the semi-frozen dessert Mother used to make with eggs and sugar and heavy cream. As a girl, I called it 'heavenly cream.' Sometimes it was made with cinnamon, chocolate, hazelnuts, or caramel." She laughed, "I couldn't eat another bite, but I wish I had some of that holiday dish! This year will be *our* first Thanksgiving together. Would you like me to make *semifreddo*? Do *you* have a favorite holiday dish?"

"Lots of time between now and then."

"True. I was just wondering what traditions we might begin as a family. This was Peyton's first summer. Next will be his first autumn. I'm actually looking forward to the cooler weather, and then his first holidays!"

"Uh, huh." Gerald was walking at a slower pace and getting farther and farther behind as she marched ahead.

She went back and reached for his hand, holding it awkwardly as they walked in the soft sand. "Anyway, I'll be glad to get home tomorrow. Seems we've been gone for so long! It was such a fun summer being here with the family. Thank you for agreeing to the joint wedding, and taking the time to stay and get to know my new/old family with me," she smiled.

"Family's good. Didn't have much. Never even met my mother's family."

"That's sad. I was an only child, so were you after your brother died. I didn't know anything about Mother's family until I found Rosalia. Mother never talked of it and refused to answer questions, only said she left it all behind and could never go back. Papa had no siblings either. His relatives were left behind in Italy. Maybe for Peyton's sake, you could try to find more of your family."

He shrugged, "Apparently they wanted nothing to do with us when folks got together. 'Mixed breeds?' Or maybe objected because so young to start a family."

"Prejudice is insidious." Mia stopped and turned to look at him. "I didn't know how much of it I harbored in myself until I met you. I couldn't have imagined being with someone not 'white,' but I wanted you. It frightened me, though you brought something undeniable to life in me."

"Literally and figuratively!" he chuckled.

Her eyes smiled up at him. "When I discovered Mother's secret and learned I wasn't white at all, I struggled with my 'changed' ethnicity! But look at me now: embracing my Mexican roots, my heritage, and also honoring how I was raised Italian like Papa."

"Lucky to experience several cultures."

She beamed. "And lucky with love! Peyton will have a potpourri of culture. And so much love!"

"True," Gerald chuckled, wrapping his arm around her as they walked back up the trail from the beach to the house.

The next day, scattered puffs of clouds obscured the view of blue sky from the window. Mia shifted the weight of Peyton sprawling across her lap on the narrow airplane seat.

"I'll take a turn." Gerald lifted him with effort.

"You're tired. You didn't sleep well?"

He shrugged. "Maybe."

Peyton squirmed and complained and commanded their attention to manage his outbursts to prevent irritating other passengers on the multiple flights.

"Ugh! Why did we fly in here?" Mia whined later as they lugged the diaper bag and baby through the Sky Harbor Airport in Phoenix.

"Said y' wanted to fly over Grand Canyon," Gerald offered as they squeezed into a booth in a café.

"'Restless Mia' longing for travel and sights unseen when I should be thinking more of toddler manageability—or lack thereof!"

Peyton grabbed a fork from the table. Gerald distracted his interest with colored photos on the menu while Mia wrestled it from his grasp. "He's getting so determined! We'll have our hands full keeping him out of trouble from now on without all the family around."

He shook his head. "Sorry. You'll be on your own; I'll be teaching."

"During the school day, but evenings are the most challenging! Why is it kids up the ante when parents are the most tired?" she sighed.

Peyton on Gerald's lap waved and flopped a paper napkin like a flag.

"I wonder how single parents work and take care of their kids, and keep sane and healthy?"

Gerald's dark eyes met hers. His voice was quiet, deliberate, "Sanity is variable, health is a gift."

Her eyes searched his round face: the crinkles at the corner of his eyes, full lips like cushions on which to fall. A sigh rose in her chest. "Health a gift..." she muttered, "I never thought of it like that. I guess it would have to be, except for the part we control with diet and exercise, positive outlook and personal habits. So you think of DNA as the gift of health we receive? Or something else?"

"Some things are mystery. Creation. Don't have control over most of it."

"Modern science is trying to gain control!"

"It can try. Some things defy explanation. Some things just are."

Mia rubbed a sudden chill from her arms.

They finished eating, and eventually loaded onto another airplane. The did fly over the Grand Canyon.

Mia stared down at the Colorado River—a blue streak through red and creamy layered land. Her mind turned to the miles of blue water of the lower Columbia River separating Oregon and Washington. Those miles led her through a rainstorm from Portland, Camas, Washougal, White Salmon, Wishram, Maryhill, over the Sam Hill Memorial Bridge to Biggs Junction, Rufus, and Gerald. Had that journey to him been coded on her DNA? Was it an internal destiny like a thread—blue like water or blood in veins—pulling her along? Did that thread of DNA also pull her like a magnet to Mexico through an incredible series of strange connections all to find the waiting arms of the mother she was missing but didn't know existed? What if she hadn't followed that pull?

Life...mystery...

Whose words were in her mind?

Gifts given...and lost...

Victoria had succumbed to cancer. If she'd fought, would it have been different? Did she know the fight was futile, prolonging suffering with no better result? Mia let out a long held breath. Two years since Mother passed, almost three since Mia had lost the last baby—Tim's baby. Now he was raising another baby of another spouse. So was she. How quickly life turns. Mia swallowed and closed her eyes on canyons below now dark with the settling sun.

Back in Seattle, Gerald launched artful lesson plans at the Ballard school, Adams Elementary. Mia tackled daily trials of keeping up with Peyton, cleaning house, and struggling with mounting frustration over lack of time and energy and adequate concentration to promote her novel, or write anything new. After dinner most nights, Gerald helped with Peyton's bedtime story and tuck-in, while Mia finished dishes and tidying the house. She'd settle down to try to read a book, but her eyes would drift over to Gerald. Her mind pondered education dilemmas, and she said,

"Low expectations are passed from generation to generation in San Bartolome Quialana. Women and girls especially aren't encouraged to learn more than basics. Mama become a business woman through her own determination and effort. Learning English was instrumental in her success. How can skills learned be translated into lessons?"

But he was plodding through countless classroom papers and did not respond.

As October was moving to a close, Mia phoned Rosalia. They chatted about the baby crawling everywhere and pulling up on furniture, Gerald's work, and other daily things like cooking. Then Mia asked, "Mama, what will you do before Christmas?"

"Go San Bartolome Quialana! *Dia De La Virgen de Guadalupe* (Our Lady of Guadalupe Day)!"

"December 12?"

"Need build for celebration. Need Javier! And man say take hunting in mountains. Javier excited! How much miss life in mountains!"

"Doesn't he like coastal life?"

"Like mountains more," Rosalia answered quietly. "Good go to San Bartolome Quialana. Miss *Abuelita*! Only few months, but heart aches."

"Our family and friends are wonderful, and fun. When you're there, do you miss your house at the beach?"

Rosalia paused, then answered, "Is life. Miss much. Always."

"Do you think the blood of ancestors, some cellular memory lingering inside us, or the land itself, calls us? Or is it spirit?"

"Ask self!"

Mia chuckled, "I do, but I hear no answers, only more questions!"

"Not for us question. Life is."

"Is that how you got through the years you waited for your sister, husband, daughter to return? You accepted there was nothing more?"

"No, no say this! More is everywhere. Not for us question what more. Only pray! Work! Sew! Every stitch a prayer. Every thread like life bring together ancestor and children. Make design. No question, only sew!"

"I wish I could create like that! Needlework doesn't seem to be one of my gifts. It's hard to settle down and do the stitches."

"Easy when heart hurt. Body stay still."

"Maybe that's the problem with my sewing! My life is too good! And I'm too busy with other things."

Rosalia only sighed, "Woman choose how create, what make for family good."

Several weeks later, after Peyton was put to bed, and Mia and Gerald collapsed on the sofa in the finally quiet living room with toys strewn about and papers Gerald had worked on covering the coffee table, they looked at each other and sighed.

"I'm tired," Mia said.

"Me, too." He reached around and was rubbing her shoulder and neck.

She breathed deeply. "That feels good! This year has been a whirlwind."

"That's for sure."

"I think we're a little worn out."

"More than a little."

She leaned over, placed her hand on his chest and her lips on his neck where the skin was smooth and soft.

He shuddered.

"How about we start now? You don't have to get up early. We'll go to bed, ease away some aches and pains..." Her voice trailed as her lips kissed up his neck.

He stood and scooped her up.

She giggled.

He carried her into the bedroom and set her down

on their bed.

They slowly unbound their bodies from clothing and found places needing a little attention, and others needing even more.

When Mia woke, odd words were in her mind. She said them over and over but was unable to fall back to sleep. Finally she got up and sat down to write.

Trees stand
and bare
and weather
and wait
Night whispers,
day yells, "We welcome you who stand and wait,
you who are not torn down, you who revive
at first fits of warm sun and dampening
through cracks and scars sprouting tender
reachlings of hope after winters of loss"

Pen still in hand, Mia studied the words on the page and sighed, "Winters of loss? Why do I write such things? I want no more of that lament!"

She glanced into the mirror of the old dressing table

she'd found in a used furniture store. It was similar to one Victoria had used many years in the house in Austin. "Oh, Mother, how I miss you. I wish you were here now. You made the holidays so beautiful. I wish you had fought to live, to stay with us." She blinked back tears. "So much we didn't say, so much more we could have given. If only we could have…"

"Have what?" Gerald asked, getting up.

"Ohhh," she shoved the paper into the drawer and turned. "A tree. We should have a huge tree this year!"

He chuckled, "Turkey day isn't even here yet."

"I know. But I want to make Christmas special and beautiful like Mother did every year."

"How do we keep decorations from Peyton?"

Mia groaned, "Ohhh. Guess that will be a problem now that he can reach up."

Gerald pulled on a clean white t-shirt and blue jeans.

Mia went to get Peyton up. "Little man, little man! What an adventure we have ahead. You'll have your first Thanksgiving! And then the Feast of *La Virgen*, Christmas, New Year's, our anniversary, your birthday…"

"Y' forgot *your* birthday," Gerald said joining them.

"Ugh! I'm such an old mother! Some women are

already grandmothers by this age. I don't know why my life had to be this way."

Gerald shrugged. "Just is."

She clutched Peyton in a hug. "A mother with wrinkles and gray hair starting! When Peyton gets old enough for school I'll be looking like his Nana!"

"Lots of sentimentality and worry today. What's this about—aging?"

She sighed. "What am I to be now?"

Gerald smiled his easy way, "Thought last night'd make y' feel like a new woman."

Mia kissed each of their cheeks. "Yes, but I don't want to wear the evidence of years on my face! I want to look fresh and pretty for my little man! And my BIG man." She kissed Gerald's lips.

"Hmmm," he groaned, arms reaching around her and Peyton.

"Don't get any ideas! Baby needs his breakfast." Mia swatted Gerald's rump and pulled away.

He went and sank heavily onto the couch, and began working on student papers. "I forgot to make coffee."

"I'll make it, anything for you, wonderful you," she said in sing-song.

While the baby babbled in the background, Mia

talked on the phone. "Mama, children need to learn. It's the most important thing for them to do short of growing! If we don't teach them skills to expand their horizons, they're doomed to the subsistence lives of ancestors!"

"Are y' talking to me?" Gerald asked.

"Talking to Mama," she replied, bringing him a large cup of coffee.

He smiled, concentrated again on the student papers.

Rosalia and Mia continued on a while until Mia said, "Peyton is spreading oatmeal and applesauce everywhere. I need to get him to the bathtub!"

"Kisses for *Bebe!*" Rosalia replied making smacking noises to the grinning boy.

"Peyton loves *Nana Lia*! That's what we're calling you as of yesterday! It'll be cute when he can say it."

"Mama good teacher!"

"Gerald, too. He's such a good dad! So calm in the midst of constant motion," Mia chuckled. "Gets a bit worn down though. I don't know how single parents do all that needs doing!"

"Nana, Papa, family help."

Mia sighed loudly, "I guess some are lucky to have family close by."

"When daughter little, have sister help. Maria good!

Maybe better mother, older. Sister say, 'Rosalia only want play with Mano!' *Ay!* Words haunt years!"

"Mama! Surely you don't blame your adolescent desires for losing me! It was Mother's evil husband, Guillermo! He was vile! He did horrible business which terrified my father. He maimed and caused irreparable harm to you and Mother! She *had* to take action against him! *He* was the cause of agony. *He, or his men*, caused her to run with me and never return to Mexico, to live her life in fear. And you alone without us."

Rosalia interjected loudly. "But even young wife know how make man do something. *I* want stay with sister. And want work for Mano. Know work of Guillermo no good, and Mano no like this work, but *I* say he must do what can for money, for family."

"There was no way to know what would happen. You've done penance for whatever wrongs you felt were done or lacks you possessed. You worked hard, and were faithful to your husband."

But Rosalia was shaking her head, "Lose faith, wish evil…"

"Oh, Mama! What wife doesn't think awful things when she suspects her husband has a new lover? I did!"

"I wish Mano *burn* in passion! Too late beg forgiveness, fire spread…"

Mia responded with loving concern, "You suffered for that! *You* were burned, burning your sin from you. You were essentially born again with Javier's care."

"True. Love and work heal."

"I believe that. After losing the babies and Tim and Mother, I doubted everything. But Gerald brought change to me. My mind and my heart opened. And then I found you."

"Love and prayers find daughter!"

"Prayers are powerful! They can settle us when we're worrying about what might come."

"No worry! Be busy. Keep love in heart. Believe!"

"You're wise, Mama. Thank you. I'd better hang up. I need to bathe *Bebe* Peyton. I love you."

As water flowed into the tub, words flowed, too.

Dragonfly

flitting over my heart

buzzing buzzing

Drown my cries

with your music

carry away my worry

Outgrowth

Thanksgiving came with a gathering of friends. Laughter and conversations filled their ears and hearts as well as scrumptious food filled their bellies.

The next day, Mia and Gerald were out early to purchase a Christmas tree they put up on a tall wooden box. While Peyton took his nap, Mia retrieved boxes of ornaments and lights from storage. Gerald prepared to go to the school while she hung the lights and ornaments on the tree.

"I wanted to do a themed décor this year, but I realized it doesn't matter. I'd rather use all Mother's ornaments Papa let me take, the ones I made last year. I so enjoyed creating them. As I painted each ornament, it felt as if I was drawing each individual to my heart. When I saw you in the grocery, I thought for a moment I had conjured your image with all my longing!"

Gerald smiled, coming over, reaching around and pulling her to him. "Y're amazingly creative. Conjuring home and family and friends seems to be y'r special talent."

She laughed, raised up and kissed his full lips.

A sigh escaped him. "Y' have a way with me, too."

"*You* have a way with *me!*" she breathed.

"We could…"

She grabbed his hand and they quietly and quickly went into the bedroom. They reached under clothes for the parts that mattered, and minutes later, were laughing.

"Glad there's still time for surprise," he grinned.

"Meaningful *moments* seem the most renewing. And the most possible with a baby in the house."

"Y' can fit a lot more of 'em in a life. Less preparation, more variety, less perfection."

She shook her head, looking over at him as they were resting on their backs on the bed. "*Better* than perfection. Before we met, I was always planning, preparing, executing with good results. But I was a little let down when tasks were finished. The work of being so precise wore me down but didn't satisfy my longing for…something."

He nodded, dark eyes on her lighter brown ones. "Y're relaxed about most things now."

"Except when I get the creepy feelings I've been having lately and don't know why."

Gerald shrugged. "Lot's changed quickly. Maybe just need to catch up with y'rself."

"Maybe."

"Or maybe feeling y'r age," he sighed. "Been feeling mine. Chasing Peyton, keeping up with school kids, class prep, teacher conferences and everything else…"

She snuggled into the space between his arm and chest, her head on his shoulder. "You *do* 'everything else' sooo *well!*"

They kissed, then resituated their clothing, and went to the kitchen. She brewed fresh coffee and they drank the steaming white and sugared brew.

"I like this," she said examining her handmade mug Gerald had purchased from a local potter. "The glaze is pretty and I like the feel of the bumpy clay."

"*This* hefty handle's just right for my big hand."

"I like what you handle," she said heavy with suggestion, and flashed him a sparkling smile.

He laughed heartily, and then they heard Peyton wake up. "Uh oh."

"Time. We used it well."

"Superbly. But, work calls. Gotta go soon."

Mia nodded, swallowed another drink, set down her cup, and went to get Peyton up. She changed his diaper and brought him out grinning. "See, baby, mama and daddy made the tree pretty. Just for looking though, not touching."

Gerald lifted Peyton up to see the ornaments. "This one's for you little man. Mama painted *you*!"

Peyton giggled and pointed to the smiling face on a gleaming red ball.

"Here is one I painted for Daddy last year," Mia said showing a gleaming ball covered with 'Gerald' and rainbows.

"Bet y' could make some money painting these."

Mia scanned the ornaments. "I've always liked painting. Though in the past, walls and furniture were the only things I painted. Oh, and displays and signs for the store Tim and I owned."

"Y're an artist," Gerald said setting down their son and watching Peyton on the floor beneath the tree.

"Thank you. I thought if I was meant to find a creative calling, I would've been 'discovered' or somehow 'known' it when I was younger."

Gerald shrugged. "Maybe y' had to be over forty to

find y'r truest self."

Peyton moved quickly across the floor to the opened storage boxes stuffed with papers. His eyes were bright with adventure as his little hands began tearing up tissues the ornaments had been wrapped in.

Mia scooped him up and kissed his chubby cheeks while carrying the resistive boy to the kitchen. She put him in the high-chair, and said in sing-song, "Say bye-bye to Daddy. He has to prepare for an event next week. After you eat, maybe we'll go take a peek. Peek!"

Peyton smiled and clapped as if playing a game.

Mia laughed, "Oh, darling boy."

Gerald's big hand rustled the boy's thick, dark hair. "Peek," he whispered in deep voice. "Daddy goes to work." He waved good-bye, and went toward the door.

Peyton pounded on his tray.

Mia sang, "Bye-bye, Daddy. Bye-bye you go. But we won't cry. You'll come back, we know!"

Peyton clapped.

"We miss you, miss you, when you're gone. Miss you, miss you, when gone too long. We will cry, but know we'll see you in the bye-and-bye."

Peyton clapped for Mia to sing again, but she was wiping away a tear. Then, she put on a smile, and sang,

"Eat, little man. Carrots and peas. Yum, yum! Please eat your carrots and peas so good for your tum tum!"

Later, while Peyton played with his toys on the floor, Mia picked up her phone and made a call.

"Hello?"

"Hi, Deena."

"How are you doing, Mia? Long time no see! Sorry to miss yesterday at your Thanksgiving. We celebrated with my parents up in Sedro-Woolley."

"We had a good time. Hope you did as well."

"Want to get together? I had a cancellation."

"Sure. Great actually."

"Let's meet at TM Dessert Works in Phinney?"

"Okay!" Mia responded with a wide grin."

"Petit fours are calling me!"

They met a short while later at the restaurant, made their selections, and settled at a table.

Mia cut into tender chocolate cake and watched creamy molten lava ooze out. She giggled, took a moist bite, and smiled. "I never tire of this taste!"

Deena popped a bite of a strawberry petit four in her mouth. "Do you let Peyton have sugar yet?"

"Not refined. But he gets plenty of other sugars,"

Mia replied peeling a fruit and holding it out for him to take.

He made a noise sounding like, "Banna! Banna!"

"Not even one year old and speaking, sort of!"

"Yes. Gerald talks to him and reads aloud. We both get an education," Mia laughed. "He loves to read history."

"Isn't it incredible? A year ago we were sitting right here, then I took you over to the house and..."

"It was such a surprise!" Mia interjected. "I had no idea Gerald had money enough to make a down payment on a house. Or even wanted to!"

"Strong men are mysterious. That proposal was so special! I was thrilled be in on the secret!"

"I had no idea! He's not withholding exactly. But he doesn't spew his thoughts. He's like a fisherman slowly letting out his line."

Deena laughed. "He caught you!"

"He did. Me and Peyton. For life."

"How are 'your' other kids? Kelsey hasn't heard from Marisol in a while."

"I'm glad they're pen-pals. I hope Kelsey keeps writing. It gives Marisol good practice with English."

Nodding, Deena added, "Cultural education is priceless for them both! I hope they'll be life-long friends.

Will the kids be coming for a visit soon?"

Mia nodded. "Benito has his check up at Seattle Children's Hospital after Christmas. I hope we can afford to bring them again in the summer. Things are a bit tight with only Gerald's salary. And I'm really not making anything from books! We could use the extra income, but technology is not my strong suit and I haven't figured out how to utilize social media for publicity," she sighed.

"Why don't you start a business? You have an eye for value and such a flair for decorating. You could buy and flip houses with Lonni and me!"

"Oh! Are you doing another house? She won't sell the beautiful one you're in will she? It's barely finished!"

"Oh, no! It's too perfect for all our needs. Kelsey and I love the apartment, and Lonni and her 'friend' are quite happy with the upstairs."

"How are you getting along with the new love?"

"Well, it was uncomfortable at first. Always takes time to get to know each other, especially with the separate living areas. But I like Stephanie. She's quite accomplished in her field: historical preservation. And of course they have architectural interests in common. But also culinary arts, and music. Steph is fiery, protective, sharp witted. The opposite of Lonni. And it was hard to see them together."

"I can imagine. Even if not jealous."

"No, I've made peace my past with Lon and the present with Lonni. And Steph's forceful personality is hard coating protecting her tender and compassionate side."

"What's her story?"

"Story?"

"Everyone has a story—what led to now."

"Oh. She shared some with me. Steph was married, had a couple kids. Indulged in alcohol and drugs. Then her husband was killed in some kind of a shooting."

"That's awful!"

"She fell deeper into it with friends who were entrenched in the lifestyle. Her daughter, who was then a young teen, was abused horribly by one of Stephanie's 'sometimes' boyfriends who also knocked her and the other kids around."

"Awful! So many terrible things happen but somehow some people find a way out and aren't bitter. I don't know how they do it! My mama, Rosalia, and her sister who raised me were raped and cut and barely escaped with me and their lives!" Tears pooled in her eyes. "I was younger than Peyton! I don't know how they escaped..."

"Wow!"

"The sisters were separated, and never saw each

other again. Growing up, I was protected from all that knowledge. And I didn't know the fear Mother harbored. I was sheltered. I came to believe bad things only happen to foolish or poor and stupid people, 'other' people. Other 'kinds' of people. I was prejudiced and narrow minded! I didn't know how people can be led astray, or have terrible things happen to them for who knows what reason out of their control," Mia said with disgust. "So much tolerance and compassion I needed to learn."

Deena nodded. "Thankfully, life provides opportunities for expanding knowledge of things beyond ourselves and our previous capabilities."

Mia took a drink, gazed on Peyton's face. "I thought educational and economic poverty caused most of life problems. But now, I realize, life is much more complex."

"*We* are complex! Sometimes I think I have people figured out, and WHAM! Something different!"

Mia chuckled. "*People* as in *man* people? Are you and Ira still dating? Are you exclusive, or dating others here and there?"

"Not formally exclusive yet. I'm not going to lie, there was a bit of possible returning intrigue with someone I dated before—Kip," Deena smiled. "He was cute! Freckles, sandy hair, beach body…"

"What happened?"

"Waves all over the world had to be conquered."

"Ohhhh. Surfer dude."

"I knew he was all wrong for me: I wanted stability and a future."

"I'd be terrible out there dating! I did date a lot in high school, but had no real or lasting relationships. Mostly crushes and infatuations."

"I did like Kip a lot. But it was months in between contacts with him." Deena shook her head and frowned. "I'm no longer willing to accept those terms: seeing someone only whenever he decides to show up."

"That would SO not work for me either! I love continuity, the daily stuff of waking side by side, cooking and eating together, even doing chores."

"I want all that now. Occasional good times aren't enough. Even a few *GREAT* times aren't either."

"True," Mia sighed, finishing her last bite of chocolate and glancing out the window at the leaden sky.

"Everything okay with you?"

"I love being home with Peyton, but Gerald puts in a lot of time with school. I guess we've been a bit tired to take on anything new and interesting lately." Mia stood, gathered up their dishes, placed them in the bussing tub while Deena played with giggling Peyton's feet.

"Think you'll ever have another child?" Mia asked watching them.

"NO! Kelsey was my miracle child. It was hard losing Lon, keeping the secret from him of making her after we broke up. But through all the difficulties getting pregnant and raising her on my own until last year, she has been so worth it! Oh, my goodness, what a child! But she's my one and only. What about you and Gerald, will try for another?"

Mia's eyes shifted from Deena to Peyton. "Oh, I don't know. Time will tell."

Peyton smeared the last of his banana on the high chair tray, then shook his sipping cup and adding drops of milk to the mess.

Mia wiped him and the tray clean. "That's it for today," she chuckled. She scooped him up, and they went out to their cars. "Was so good seeing you!"

"Think about making some changes. Maybe you could set a time limit and make a daily habit of writing," Deena suggested as they hugged good-bye.

"I feel on the brink of change. Maybe something different is about to come along. Something..." she shrugged. "Thank you for the 'sweet' visit!"

As Mia drove back toward her house, words were in her mind.

Outgrowth—

a baby—

seed spun out into the world

separate

capable

free

Now what about me?

Splitting

As Christmas approached, the days were getting shorter and darker with cloudy and rainy skies. Nearly every evening was filled with holiday festivities, and whenever possible, they lingered as long as possible in the bed as morning rose. The house was quiet. There were no sounds on the street outside. Maybe the whole world was still.

Mia huddled under the covers and snuggled up to Gerald's backside.

There was no response from him.

Her hand touched his shoulder: warm fingers on cool skin.

"Ger?" She shook his shoulder.

He was still.

"Gerald?" Her voice raised, "Gerald!" She pulled him onto his back, felt his neck, grabbed her phone and called 911, ran to unlock the front door, started CPR.

Sirens pealing through the neighborhood broke the morning quiet as vehicles sped up with colored lights flashing.

EMT's rushed in.

"We'll take over, Ma'am," they said crowding into the bedroom, and removing her from Gerald.

Mia backed up to the doorway, frozen there with hands gripping the woodwork.

Protocols were followed.

More sirens. Police officers entered.

"Ma'am, can you tell us what happened?"

"What happened? What happened?" she echoed, dry eyed. "We were sleeping. Everything was so quiet. I said something, but he didn't answer. I touched his shoulder. His skin was cold! He's so cold! Why is he so cold?" She started shivering.

Someone brought her a blanket.

Mia stared into the bedroom. "What day is it?"

"Shortest day of 2009: December 21," a voice said.

Mia's eyes moved to the window. Someone had opened the curtains. Outside, fog encapsulated the house. "What can help him? Can you do something to warm him?"

No one said anything in response. Cries sounded from the other bedroom, but Mia couldn't move from her post at the door.

Peyton was carried to her. She buried her face in his neck, the warm soft place still sweet with sleep. "Pey-Pey, it's a short day, short day," she whispered again and again like a song, the baby giggling with her breath on his skin.

Someone led her to the kitchen, made coffee for her. She fed Peyton oatmeal and peaches, fetched a warm cloth to wash his face and hands. She paused, suddenly noticing the front door closing. "What's happening? Who's leaving? Is he better?" She started for the bedroom.

A hand gripped her arm.

She turned to stare.

A man's face. Angular. Clean shaven. Head shiny. Pale skin. Blue eyes looking at her. "Ma'am, I'm sorry."

Her eyes were round as if not blinking could suspend time, stop anything from happening.

"The coroner will need to make a determination. Did the deceased have a history of health problems?"

Her eyes jumped to the half-dozen professionals

packing up equipment. "History? He loved history."

"A medical history?"

"Gerald said his father passed at an early age. A smoker. Drinker. Heart attack I think."

"Your husband a drinker? Smoker?"

"No," she whispered. "He's healthy. He never complains. Except when he's tired." Her brow furrowed.

"Ma'am, did your husband make his wishes known?"

She was shaking her head, distracted by Peyton. She plucked him from the high-chair, but stood immobile in the middle of the kitchen.

"Someone you can call to take care of the baby?"

She nodded slowly, set Peyton in a playpen in the living room, picked up her phone, made a call.

"Susan? It's Mia; I need you. Can you come? Right now? Will you…" she paused, swallowed. "Call your mom. Ask Joyce to…Tell her it's…Gerald." She wiped her hand across her sweating brow though she was shivering, too. Her voice was shaking. "I need her. Ask her if she can come from Austin right away, OK? Tell her to call Papa…"

"I can watch the boy a bit if you'd like to take a few moments to yourself," a woman in uniform said smiling at Peyton, and began showing him toys.

Mia studied the interaction a moment, kissed Peyton's dark head of hair, went into the bathroom and closed the door. The shower started. Her voice sounded over the running water, "What happened? What happened?"

A short time later, Mia came out re-dressed in her pajamas, her hair in a single braid still dripping water down her back. She stood in the bedroom doorway.

"Ma'am, we're finished here. You can dress him if you want, but there's no need at this point."

She remained motionless.

"You can have a few minutes with him. But we need to supervise. I'm sorry. Procedure."

She sat on the edge of the bed. Her fingers traced each brow, the crinkles at the corner of his eyes, his smooth cheeks. She stroked his broad, smooth chest, and shoulders, and neck, placed a kiss on his lips—lips once cushioning like a pillow on which to fall, now still and cool and unmoving.

She might have thrown back the covers, might have examined every inch of him with love and longing and tears in her eyes, but she only leaned down and whispered in his ear, "Ger, what happened? What happened? What will happen now? Tell me what to do about this…" A splitting pain seared through her, taking her breath.

Someone took her hand, led her to the kitchen and poured her another cup of coffee. Maybe she told them to add sugar and cream, for it was sweet and white. She drank it down slowly with hands clutching the handmade ceramic mug Gerald liked as the gurney was wheeled out the door.

Susan arrived and helped with Peyton all day. They had just finished getting him to bed in the evening when Joyce arrived via taxi. She came in out of the rain, set down her luggage. Susan hugged her mother and hung up Joyce's dripping coat. Joyce went over to the kitchen table where Mia was using a #2 pencil with worn down eraser to write on ruled paper covered in little bits of rubber and smeared lead. Joyce stood at Mia's side but did not touch her.

"Don't say anything," Mia said quietly.

Joyce and Susan exchanged glances.

"Have you eaten, Mom? Mia wasn't hungry, but I made some chicken soup."

"That sounds good," Joyce answered and dished up some from the stove, then sat down at the table.

"Will you look over what I've written?" Mia asked.

"Sure. While *you* eat."

"I can't," Mia replied, standing up and turning toward the bedroom. "I need to lie down for a bit."

"Need help freshening it up?"

"*No*! It's fine how it was."

"Of course," Joyce replied calmly.

"Thank you for coming," Mia said in nearly a whisper. She retraced her steps and reached out stiffly to pat Joyce's shoulder as if a hug was just too close, or might crush her.

"Get some rest. We'll be here."

Mia closed the bedroom door.

Joyce and Susan talked quietly.

Clothes stripped off and dropped in a heap on the floor, Mia slipped into the bed of cool sheets. Resting her head on Gerald's pillow, she turned her face to the smooth pillowcase and breathed in his scent.

"Ger…" she whispered. "What happened to you?" Something knifed through her. "Mama, is this the pain you felt when Mano was gone? How did this happen? I have to see him again…" Mia sobbed so hard the bed shook and she ran a hand over her eyes and looked for the source of the movement. Prayers fled from her lips—prayers for light to sweep her up in a swirling backward motion of time.

He was beside her, facing away, his
breathing rhythmic.

"Ger…" she whispered. Her hand

reached out to him, warm fingers gliding over
smooth skin.

His breathing changed. He sighed,

turning toward her.

"You make me feel something," she

whispered.

"I feel something," he grinned, arms

pulling her to him, skin to skin.

"Ger..." she whispered.

Mia squeezed the vision from her crying eyes and prayed
harder, but her prayers were questions, pleas. "What hap
pened? What will happen to us? We were making our own
traditions to celebrate all the years ahead. We were planning our first anniversary next month, Peyton's birthday.
We were making so many plans. What am I to do now without our plans? How will I get through the days and the
nights and more days and more nights..."

A light was shining when Mia opened her eyes again, but it
was only faint light of morning coming in through the open
curtains.

Her mind traced every word and sight and sound of
yesterday—the shortest day of the year—followed by the

long night of strange dreams.

Gerald's scent still lingered on his pillow. The mattress wore a slight indent where he had slept many nights. Clothes he had worn were in the hamper; his toothbrush was in a cup next to the sink. Long strands of his dark hair were twined around the bore bristles of the brush he used. Papers with his handwriting were on student papers. Pans he had washed by hand were still resting in the dishrack, groceries he bought still waiting to be consumed.

Mia silently shed tears, then unable to remain still any longer, she got up, showered, dressed, and went out to the kitchen where Joyce was feeding Peyton.

"Get coffee," Joyce commanded softly, her green eyes sleepy but her voice capable, strong.

Peyton jabbered at Mia and slapped his spoon to the high chair tray.

"Yes, Pey-Pey, I'm here." Mia kissed his hair and breathed in his baby scent.

"Dadadada."

"Ohhhh." Tears filled her eyes. "He's too little to understand." Mia glanced at Joyce. "Gerald's not gone. We just don't see him."

Susan turned from the sink dishes.

"You think I'm wrong?"

"No, no we don't. Not at all," Susan offered gently. "I felt that way when my dad died."

"Yes," Joyce said. "When the unthinkable happens, everyone has a different way of coping with loss."

"It's a change, not a loss really. It's just a change in perception."

"Um, okay, sure. I get that. You're saying he's still here in a way."

"Yes," Mia nodded. "Just different."

Joyce sighed, "I felt that when Neil passed. For a while."

"How long?" Mia barely whispered, her shaking hands pouring coffee into a cup.

"Weeks. Months maybe. Off and on for years. Sometimes, his side of the bed felt warm, as if he'd just left it. Sometimes I could hear his laughter in the house. It's what I missed most of him. I didn't laugh anymore. That part of me went away, too, for a while."

Mia nodded dully.

"We had shared so many great and funny times. We were always joking and talking."

"That sounds nice: noise and laughter. We don't joke much," she gulped down the coffee. "I guess we're quiet people." Mia refilled her cup, added cream and sugar.

"Thank you both for staying. Hope you weren't miserable on the sofa bed."

Joyce smiled, "It wasn't bad. What do we need to do today?"

Shrugging, Mia answered, "I'll set up the memorial at the school for the 27th."

"Doesn't give much time to prepare."

She nodded. "School will still be out. The 31st is the full moon..." Mia's brow furrowed. "I dreamed the moon, white as snow shining down like a search light. I don't know what that meant..." She looked at her hands. "Our friend, Ira, at the paper in Ballard, can put together an article. And maybe Lonni and Stephanie and Deena will host a brunch at their house after the service."

"That would be nice," Joyce responded kindly.

Peyton was cleaned up and let loose from the high chair. He crawled all over the house for more than an hour while they worked on household chores.

Mia sat down to finish writing on the article for Ira. Finally pushing it away, she rubbed her eyes. "Probably time for Peyton's morning nap. I'll lay down with him."

"Okie dokie. We'll prepare something for dinner. Any requests?"

"Parmesan chicken? Noodles, steamed broccoli?"

"Perfect," Joyce smiled.

Mia carried Peyton over to them for hugs.

Joyce and Susan gave kisses. "Nappy nap!"

"Thank you," Mia smiled.

"Here to serve," Joyce said cheerfully. "Let us know what else you need."

Mia smiled wistfully and nodded before turning into her bedroom and shutting the door.

Susan whispered, "Is she okay?"

"It's a lot to take in. Probably in emotional shock. Parts of the mind shut down."

"Is that how you were when dad died?"

"No. We had years of worry and struggle and hope and disappointment, many ups and downs with his cancer treatment. In the end, he was ready to let go. As hard as it was to see death come, it was peaceful. This is quite something different. Shocking, and unexplained at this point. Tough to make sense of it."

"Mia *seems* strong though."

"That could change at any point when her emotions come back to fullness. Time will show what true strength is." Joyce looked through the cupboards for ingredients and equipment for preparing the dinner. "Shall we make the noodles from scratch?"

"Do you roll out the dough with a pin and board?"

"Could, but let's try using the pasta roller I found."

"Oh, cool!" Susan smiled.

"Let's bake a dessert, too. I think I have a recipe or two in my head."

"Oh, mom! You don't have to try to remember anything. Just look it up online."

"HA! I guess we could!"

They chattered quietly while preparing the dough and vegetables and chicken.

"Weren't Angelo and Maggie going on a Christmas cruise to celebrate how they met two years ago?"

"Their plans changed."

"Sad they live so far away in Austin."

"*I'm* that far away!"

"I know," Susan answered. "I wish you weren't. I needed my independence for a while. But now I miss you more."

"Awww," Joyce smiled, her eyes misty. "Mia didn't spend much time at all with her family after she married Tim and moved to Oregon. They've only been close since Mia's divorce."

"What about her grandmother in Austin?"

"Angelina? Maybe she'll come with Angelo and

Maggie; hope so. I always enjoy her," Joyce chuckled. "She has such dignity and composure, but we're beginning to melt her reserve. When we were in Mexico for the weddings, she told me to call her 'Grandmother.'"

"That's sweet! Such a small family. Glad ours was bigger, and you had two of us kids."

Joyce smiled, "You and David were good kids, but you're even better adults!"

"Geez, I just now wondered if Mia and Gerald would have another baby," Susan sighed, tears in her eyes.

"Oh," Joyce frowned. "I don't know if they were thinking they would have more children. It was a shock to have *any* after Mia had difficulty conceiving with her first husband, and several miscarriages and a baby lost closer to term. Mia had been told it'd be extremely unlikely she'd carry any baby to birth, even if she could get pregnant."

"I guess Peyton really is a miracle," Susan sighed.

Later, they had a laugh over the fat noodles Joyce and Susan made, but the pasta was tasty. Peyton enjoyed stuffing handfuls into his mouth. The apple crisp was perfect with vanilla ice cream. After all dishes were cleaned, Mia said, "I'm sure you could use better sleep at Susan's tonight."

"That's true," Joyce hesitated.

"I'm okay. If there's anything…"

"Call! We'll come back fast!" they said and hugged good-bye.

Once Peyton was settled in bed for the night, Mia stripped off her clothes. She stepped into a very hot bath in the claw foot tub like the one Gerald had at his little cabin near Rufus, Oregon. Those weeks with him at the beginning of summer two and a half years ago had been respite from everything her life had been up to that point. She'd left there without meaning to, but he found her again a year later in Texas. And they found each other again months later in Seattle. Would there ever be another finding?

Water dripped from her face. Maybe it was steam condensing on her cool skin. A cycle. Life's cycle.

Mia sighed. A year ago she'd sent Marisol and Benito on a plane back to Mexico with Rosalia and Javier. "How did I find the strength to let them all go?"

She closed her eyes. Her mind drifted back to that day. "I felt such sadness I thought I couldn't rise from the depths again. But the next day when I woke, I knew I had to go out and face the day—even if alone."

Tears rolled down her face. "I walked and walked, and went to Ken's Market. As I looked at the luscious produce, I suddenly did not feel alone. Goodness was with me.

I looked up and you were standing across the way and smiling. How I loved you in that moment. If I hadn't had the sadness of the day before, I wouldn't have gone out to the store, we wouldn't have found each other again."

"I lost babies, lost Tim to Valerie. Was brought from the edge by you. I lost Mother, my Italian heritage, everything I thought was my life until then. But, I found my Mexican roots and Mama."

Mia whispered, "Depths of pain followed by gifts of joy. Oh, Blessed Mother, why didn't you tell me of these *suffering gifts*?"

"Is it also the other way—suffering *after* great gifts? If that's true, I'll dread every good thing for losses to follow," she cried pushing herself out of the tub. After toweling dry, Mia slipped on a robe, and went to her laptop.

> How I long for you
>
> and wish you come
>
> How I wait for your embrace
>
> My heart aches with longing
>
> to hear you
>
> touch you

> linger in your long looks
>
> melting me
>
> glacier ice
>
> streaming
>
> catching us in the flow

Those were the words written a year ago before going out alone to the store, and finding Gerald there.

> Words spell out exact miseries
>
> Words bring clarity.
>
> Words can comfort

"Tell me something. Tell me what to do…"

She searched the internet for poems about loss, grief, love—so many words and images and videos and music for filling an empty heart.

"I'm not alone in it," she whispered.

Mia opened an account on **Pinterest** and began pinning to a board, "*Beautiful words and images for the beleaguered.*"

Humidity

Next morning; Mia was up and out early to Golden Gardens Park in Ballard. She pushed Peyton in the stroller down a path. Rain was threatening but not falling. The Olympic Mountains stood witness to water and sky.

She wore the red dress worn for their wedding here last winter, the dark trench coat, and black rubber boots. Peyton was bundled in the brightly patterned wool blanket Mia had first seen over two years ago on Charlotte's couch when visiting Gerald's grandmother near The Dalles. This morning she found it in the closet. Instead, she might have wrapped Peyton in Gerald's old black quilt with stitches spiraling over fading colors of blue and yellow and red.

Many nights she traced a finger round and round until sleep found her. She and Gerald had first found each other beneath that cover of cotton. But the quilt on the bed was soft and old and could not weather more than storms of emotion.

Now she paused on the path to point out sailboats with sails in those same colors: red, yellow and blue, skimming across Puget Sound. "See Peyton? All the little boats are sailing somewhere far, far, and away."

He grinned and clapped.

She pushed the stroller down the paved pathway and wet wheels squealed in a kind of music. Wind was at her back, nudging. And words formed in her mind.

> I know you are with me
> A comfort in storm
> Warm sun break through clouds
> You shine

Mia glanced up to grey clouds. "And I'll remember, even when I don't see them, the sun and moon and stars are still there, still shining. I'll remember you are there."

Just then, Peyton pointed at two ducks gliding to a landing on the water. "Dada! Mama!"

"Yes, darling. But they have no little duckling. They are not as lucky as us!" She tucked a dangling blanket edge and patted his cheek. "This is a special place for Daddy and me. I wanted you to see it today. But now, it is time to go back to our nest, my Little Duck."

They soon were home and eating lunch, and then Peyton went for a nap. Wrapped in Gerald's old quilt, Mia settled down on the sofa. Stalks of summer flowers now dry and crisp rattled against the window. She might have drifted to sleep while everything was quiet and her mind was hazy like dreaming. But a knock at the door startled her. She opened it to a line of people filing in. Tears slipped down her cheeks as she greeted them with quick hugs.

"We're your extended family! Couldn't let your birthday go by unnoticed."

"Thank you, Joyce, all of you! I'm touched. Really. I'm surprised you remembered."

Looks were exchanged.

"We had help," Deena replied.

Kelsey chimed, "Gerald planned it for you."

"I wish he was here," Lonni said quietly.

They all smiled through tears.

"He wanted you to have the birthday party you've been missing all these years," Joyce managed to say.

Eyes were wiped, hands busied unpacking bags and unwrapping dishes.

"I wish Marisol and Benito were here, too!" Kelsey blurted.

"Me, too," Mia answered. "But Peyton will be awake soon. You can play with him."

"We brought something to give him! Could it be an early Christmas?" Kelsey asked.

"Sure."

"We had various ideas for supper. Spaghetti won," Deena said.

"All hands on deck for prep!" Stephanie, Lonni's partner commanded.

"Dibs on garlic bread," Lonni said raising a hand. "That's easy right? Slice and butter?"

"We need to make the bread first," Susan laughed.

"I could use some dough therapy," Mia said.

"Deena on sauce? Ira on salad?"

"After the dough is rising, Mia, we can go over the article?" Ira suggested.

"Yes, we've worked on it," she said while fetching bowls, cutting boards and knives, rolling pin and ingredients for the bread. She slipped on a flowered apron.

"Pretty! Like a garden," Kelsey smiled.

"Reminds me of the flowered head cloth Mother wore on hair coloring day, and like they wear in her home village."

"Rosalia?"

"Rosalia is my *real* mother, my Mama. When I was a baby, not even as old as Peyton, a tragic situation forced a separation. Rosalia's sister, Maria—I knew as Victoria—left Mexico with me, and married Angelo in Texas. They raised me as their own Italian girl. Until last year, I didn't know I had other parents, or that I was from Mexico."

"Wow!" Kelsey replied. "I'm glad I'm not the only one here with an un-normal upbringing. My dad, Lon, became Lonni and has a girlfriend. Now I have three moms!"

Lonni and Deena exchanged looks with Stephanie, and they all burst out laughing.

"Rosalia was the woman I'd been hearing in my mind for many years. I was shocked to find her!"

"*I* was there! What an adventure we had in Mexico," Joyce said. "We didn't know exactly what to look for or where. We followed clue after clue in and around Oaxaca City, and when we could find nothing sure, we gave up and went to the beach in Puerto Escondido. And that's where a bright spot shining through the trees lured Mia. She followed a light straight to the woman she did not know she was missing! It was one of the most magical things I've ever witnessed."

"How did Gerald fit into the picture?" Ira asked.

Mia paused in dough preparation. "The summer before that, Gerald saved me from a deadly fall from a cliff."

Deena stopped chopping tomatoes. "I have not heard this! What were you doing on a cliff?"

"Ohhh, that's a long story," Mia sighed.

"You don't have to talk about it," someone said.

But Mia shook her head. "Maybe you all know I was married fifteen years to Tim. We met at college in Austin. He was a business major, had opportunity to buy a jewelry and gift store in Portland. We'd only dated a few months, but he seemed to be everything I could look for in a husband, and I wanted to make a new life. Texas was where I'd grown up, but it didn't feel like 'home.' I didn't know why. And I felt controlled by Mother's overprotection and constant monitoring of my life."

"Mothers can do that," Susan chuckled smiling at Joyce who raised a spoon and made a funny face.

"Now I know why," Mia added. "She feared for our safety and had dangerous secrets."

"More than the secret you were taken from your mother?"

"Mother's husband was a rapist, mutilator."

"Oh, my!" gasped the crowd.

Mia continued in dramatic tone, "Mother made sure he could hurt no one again! She ran to keep us safe. Something prevented her from meeting back up with her sister, and they did not even know if each was alive."

"How terrible!"

"I was small and in such dire circumstances, losing parents I didn't really know I'd lost..." Mia's eyes filled with tears. "I wonder if Peyton will remember Gerald?"

"You remembered something..." Joyce said kindly. "You were drawn to Mexico, followed clues..."

"I guess I knew something—enough to write the novel, *Mending Stone*, which I discovered is close to what actually *is* the truth of my life!"

"Amazing!"

"How did you make the transition from running the gift store in Portland to novel writing?"

Mia paused in kneading the dough. She looked around at the rapt faces. "Tim and I worked hard to build a business, remodel a house, eventually tried to start a family. But I struggled to conceive. And then when I did...Oh. I'm sorry, Kelsey. Is it too much to hear?"

Kelsey flipped her wrist, "I know all about that!"

Everyone chuckled.

"Anyway, after miscarriages and losing a baby further along I fell into depression. I couldn't seem to recover and I was having strange dreams about a woman, a family, a baby in another country."

"Was it your mother?" Kelsey's eyes were wide.

"*Now* I know it, but back then I was just confused and upset. And I wasn't the best wife..."

"Oh, my gosh!" Joyce interjected loudly. "Your HUSBAND wasn't there for you. He was too busy making eyes at the little gal he hired to help at the store!"

Mia smiled, eyes shining with gratefulness. "Thank you, Joyce, my defender! I discovered Tim with Valerie and—after busting up the store—I ran, drove hours in a rainstorm toward nowhere I knew. After my car broke down, I found myself on a ridge high above a river. I could have been blown over to certain death, if not for Gerald."

"How'd he get there?"

"Just like a guardian angel!" Kelsey said excitedly!

"Seemed he just appeared. He heard my car break down in the quiet country and came to help, followed me up the hillside, and caught me before I went over the edge."

"Wow! That gave me chills! You were saved!"

"Twice! First by your aunt, then Gerald."

Eyebrows knitted, Mia sighed, "When I met Gerald, it felt as if something momentous had happened, as if some clog in me was freed in the most unlikely terrain of rocks and sagebrush, sand and sun. And..."

Looks went around the group, waiting.

"Gerald was steady. So sure of himself. But I thought he had not much of a life there so far from a city and the life I knew. But there *was* something. Maybe in the wind, or the water, or sky. It was unexpected and welcome. I tried to believe it was the place and time making me feel something. I didn't want it to be him."

She glanced around. "I'm ashamed to say, I thought I was Italian, upper class, 'white.' I made judgements. I didn't know stereotypes colored my life, limited my joy, narrowed my view of the world and what love I allowed."

"I know something about that," Deena said with a nod to Lonni. "Once we open to who we *really* are, we can't be the same together, or separate, any more."

"We all have limitations we fight," Lonni offered with generous smile. "I wasn't born the woman I felt I was. But fortunately, I was able to become her. Even though I'm no longer Deena's man Lon, we're friends, parents."

"Good," Kelsey said. Then added, "And strange."

Everyone laughed.

"I didn't know everything I thought about myself was a lie! It was as if I had been asleep in my own life. I woke up with Gerald!"

Deena blinked back tears. "Gerald was so ever-present, connected somehow—to something."

"Yes," Ira offered. "I thought that right away. He was real in a rare way."

Mia shaped her bread dough and placed it in a weathered bowl to rise beneath a faded cotton cloth. "I hear Peyton. Better go get my boy up." She left the kitchen.

Quick actions with lots of scurrying ensued while she was out of the room changing the baby. When Mia returned a few minutes later, she exclaimed, "Oh, my goodness! Peyton! Look! Balloons!"

He giggled and clapped.

Everyone took turns playing with the gift Kelsey brought for him to open, a big ball he tried to roll to them.

When the bread was baked, the meal was served: salad, and pasta with a vegetarian sauce and one with meatballs. Dessert was ice cream and cake. Then, with Peyton's help, Mia opened other brightly wrapped gifts: an assortment of organic lavender scented scrubs and lotions.

"Thank you! So lovely. I'm glad you're all here." Mia said, her eyes moistening.

"We weren't sure if we should," Lonni offered.

"I've never felt so loved," she said softly. "And I thank you for playing with Peyton. You wore him out! He looks sleepy. Maybe will go early to bath and bed."

"Good idea," Stephanie piped with others nodding..

The group soon left after many hugs and tears.

Susan had gone out to the car with their things while Joyce lingered. "Have any plans tomorrow?"

Mia shrugged, but said quietly, "Maybe midnight Mass."

"Early in the day I'll be ready for anything you want or need. Later, we'll be having supper with Susan and her boyfriend and family."

"Oh, gooood," Mia yawned. "Sorry. I do want to hear all about them soon."

"Talk later. We have time."

But shaking her head, Mia said, "That's what *I* thought! A whole long life of time for more of everything! I didn't know we already had everything we would have!"

"I'm so sorry, Mia. Geez! It's still beyond belief! When Neil passed, we had time to prepare. Not that one is ever ready for losing, but the idea of it happening has at least been considered."

"The shock of it..." she choked down a sob. "I can't

quite believe Gerald has gone anywhere more than a long trip. I feel him still here, even though I can't see or touch him!" She wiped away tears. "Sorry, I don't want to wallow in this."

"Wallow as long as you need. I'll be here to listen, or help in any way possible. We all will."

Mia walked Joyce to the door. "Thank you. I love you, 'Sage of the Cafeteria.'"

Joyce laughed. "Love you, too, Sister. Call me to-morrow, if only to let me know how you're doing." Joyce hugged her good-bye, and then waved while getting into Susan's car, and they drove away.

Mia shut the house door with a decisive thud.

After Peyton's bath, she rubbed lavender lotion onto his skin, and dressed him in red fleeced and footed pajamas. He snuggled in Mia's arms as she rocked him to sleep.

Tub filled again with hot water, Mia soaked, then washed and conditioned her hair, scrubbed her skin until it was red. She dried off, and smoothed lotion over every inch of her body. With her hair still wrapped in a dry towel, she slipped into the bed.

She gripped Gerald's pillow, inhaled deeply. Sleep came with dreams of running after a figure in the rain. A sound rang in her ears and footsteps pounded the ground.

"Wait! Don't go," she cried aloud.

There was a loud rapping.

Mia turned in the bed, waking but foggy with sleep.

Another rap sounded from the front door.

She got up, unwound the towel from her damp hair, pulled on a thick terry robe, and snuck to the window. She peeked out, then jerked open the door. "Papa," she sobbed, wrapping her arms around him.

"I'm sorry, Darling, to be so late. We wanted to get here in time for your party, but our flight was delayed."

She pulled them inside, and shut the door. "I thought you were on your anniversary trip."

"Actually. We lied about the timing. We have a few days in San Antonio. Don't tell Mother! She would have wanted to go! And she wanted to come here but…"

"Oh, no! What's wrong with Grandmother?"

"Nothing new. She's slowing down. The trip was just too much for her right now."

"I probably look a fright." Mia pushed back her dark hair now wavy and wild. "Sit for a moment; I'll be right back." She went into the bedroom and dressed in soft lounging pants, a long sweater, and slippers. Returning, she waved them from the couch to the table. "Let's have cake!"

Maggie helped serve while Mia fetched milk and

juice from the refrigerator and filled glasses. "I can make coffee or tea if you'd rather."

"No, no, Darling. This is fine. Stop fussing over us."

"I can make up the sofa bed for you quick."

"Thank you, Mia. That's very sweet. We thought arriving so late, perhaps a hotel for tonight would be better. We booked a room at the Ballard Hotel," Maggie replied.

"Oh, I hear it's pretty nice."

"Seemed so in their advertisements," Angelo said. "But tomorrow night perhaps we can stay over here."

"Oh, Papa! Really?" She looked one to the other.

"Yes, if you don't mind."

"You'll be here Christmas morning! I'm thrilled!"

"We wanted to be here for your birthday and Christmas," Angelo said looking down at a bite of cake on his fork. "We haven't spent both together since you left home." His eyes met Mia's. "We missed so much all the years you were with Tim in Portland. Time with family is so very precious," Angelo said blinking back tears. "We're deeply saddened by the loss of Gerald. We didn't know how short our time together was to be. We wish we'd gotten together more this year."

Mia nodded, chewing a bite of cake and swallowing with difficulty. "I know," she sighed, with eyes gleaming.

"I can't believe it's true, though my mind remembers. I can't think about it. My heart might jump right out of my skin."

"Poor Darling."

"You know we really cared about Gerald," Maggie managed to say.

"So likeable," Mia smiled. "When I first woke in his cabin on the Columbia River Gorge, I was frightened. I didn't know what had happened. I remembered staring down at the river, and the wind coming up. Then I was in the cabin with Gerald coming toward me. I wanted to get out of there! He was tall and big, but when he spoke there was something in his voice. The gentleness in his spirit, and the look of him—deep brown eyes and long, dark hair— warmed me to the core."

"A beautiful man," Maggie agreed.

"Yes," Mia breathed, nodding.

Their plates were empty but emotion hung in the air.

"We'd better let you get some rest. Call us in the morning. We can make plans then."

"Papa, could we go to midnight Mass on Christmas Eve?"

Angelo glanced at Maggie, then back to Mia. "Yes, if you like, Darling. Is there a parish you have attended?"

"No, not at all. But I'd like to go."

"Let's figure it out tomorrow."

Maggie and Angelo got up, pulled on their coats.

"Sorry it's so rainy and cool here," she said.

"It's refreshing."

"Hopefully it'll be dry for Christmas…" she sighed.

"Good to be together, no matter what."

Mia hugged and kissed them good-night. She went back to bed, and somehow slipped quickly into slumber.

Ocean

A caress, the slightest brush of a heavy hand over her hair, woke Mia in the early light of morning.

Tears sprang into her eyes. "I felt you!" she cried. "Why can't I see you! I miss you. Oh, Gerald."

But then Peyton roused and cried. Mia dried her tears, and went to get him up. She made coffee—strong and white and sweet just how Gerald always made it for her. Peyton had his usual oatmeal with fruit while she sipped and watched out the window as the world came alive with daylight.

Cars swished up and down the street and the smell of heavy rain outside seeped into the house. "Oh, Pey-Pey, what will we do with winter?"

"Dada," he answered.

"I know darling. Dada went to the bye-and bye."

Peyton frowned and pounded his spoon on the tray.

"We'll call Nana Lia soon. I tried yesterday but could not get through. I'm sure she'll be anxious to talk to you." Mia wiped his face and hands and the gooey tray before giving him a handful of Cheerios to snack on. "Let's try right now." She made the call. "Mama. I…"

"So sorry for heavy heart, miss Gerald."

"I feel him here still."

Rosalia sighed, "Make sure okay."

"Native Americans believe the spirit stays four days or more before their soul goes on another journey."

"Come soon. Hug daughter."

"Yes, just a few more days, just like we planned," she sighed with a little catch in her throat.

"Time go fast. When go back, have big change."

"What?"

"Javier show house for example build, but man want this house. And pay great price."

"You can't sell the house Javier built for you!"

"Husband build good. Make another."

"Where?"

"San Bartolome Quialana. This time, Marisol, Benito, *Abuelita* and family say come back to live."

"Will Javier have enough work there?" Mia asked with concern. "Will you be able to run your business?"

"Have idea! Javier build center. Teach sew and how make building. Maybe more. Maybe all age student."

"That's a good idea. But such a huge task! Where will you get enough money? You're not making THAT much money on the house are you?"

"Friend work government. Say maybe money for business—teach skills to native women and children. Need some time for make application."

"Sounds like you're seriously considering the venture. I'm shocked to learn this now."

"When hear of Gerald, forget this. So sorry."

Mia glanced out the window at hazy yellowed lights of cars passing by on the street. "I'm happy for you. But my heart is hurting too much to imagine these changes."

Rosalia insisted, "*La Virgen* listen. *Madre* help."

"What will you do Christmas tomorrow?"

"Celebration. And pack for trip see daughter!"

But Mia sighed, "Puerto Escondido is wonderful. Won't you miss the ocean if you move inland?"

"Time change. Life change."

Peyton fussed and reached for the phone. Mia held it up for him to listen.

"Nana Lia here, Peyton!" Rosalia chimed.

He grinned.

Mia blinked back tears. "You're so sweet, Mama."

"My heart break for daughter."

"Thank you," Mia managed to say. "Love you."

When the call ended, she reached down and brought her son to her lap. Rocking him in her arms, she sang, "Mama's here, Mama's here, Mama's here, Mama's here."

Peyton's eyes closed.

"Oh, baby," she sighed. "What are we to do? The house is too quiet." Mia tucked him into the stroller with a blanket, and dressed herself for weather. They went out into the rain. She pulled up the stroller canopy to keep him dry, and walked. Wind blew the hood from her head, but she left it. Rain soaked her hair, dripped down her face and mixed with water streaming from her eyes. Walking, walking, walking through neighborhoods, her feet slapped the pavement.

Wandering the aisles in Ken's Market in Phinney, Mia drew deep breaths and lingered in the produce section, her hands and eyes examined the shapes and colors, and her cheeks flushed. She looked quickly around, but her eyes saw no one familiar. "I feel you," she whispered from the spot where she and Gerald had reconvened only a year ago. Nothing moved.

After purchasing cinnamon sticks, milk, cream, and chocolate—ingredients for Mexican hot chocolate—she pushed Peyton toward home. He roused along the way and she fed him a squeeze package of pears and a bottle he could hold. The rain let up. With the stroller canopy down, he watched with contented quiet as they wound along.

Back at the house, Mia made the hot chocolate with the purchased ingredients plus vanilla and a dash of cayenne pepper. She sipped it slowly while Peyton ate lunch and played on the floor with his toys.

The phone rang and she answered, "Hello?"

"How are you doing?"

"Hi, Joyce. We're having a quiet day. Went for a walk. About to call Papa and Maggie. What a surprise that was!"

Joyce's voice rang with mirth. "It all would have been such an awesome gift Gerald wanted to witness."

"I think he saw and heard. He's still here," she said with quiet conviction.

"Do you feel the need of company?"

"No. I want quiet. Have a lovely Christmas Eve, and

Christmas; I'll catch up with you the day after."

There was a pause, and then Joyce said, "You know I'm here if you want or need anything, just call."

"I will, thank you. Talk to you soon."

Maggie and Angelo came over in the late afternoon. They made shrimp and grits, arugula salad and sourdough bread. After Peyton's bath, story, and tuck-in, they relaxed in the living room with caramel corn and peppermint schnapps while watching *White Christmas*.

"I love movies! I have more you can watch while we're gone, Maggie. We'll have to leave by nine o'clock to get there in time. I'd better get ready."

Mia returned some minutes later in a black dress with lace cuffs, hem, and insets. Her hair was in a single braid in back. Small diamond studs gleamed in her ears.

"What a vision you are, Darling."

"Thank you, Papa."

"Lovely dress."

"Not inappropriate for Midnight Mass?"

Angelo shook his head. "It's appropriate for any evening event."

"Even for a woman who is…"

"Love is beautiful. Marriage is beautiful. You do

them both honor by shining your light even with loss."

"Papa! You are becoming such a poet in your..."

He laughed interrupting, "In my what? Older years?"

"Yes." Mia smiled. "And doing it handsomely! Maggie are you sure you'll be okay here? I'll keep my phone on vibrate; we can hurry back if needed. Peyton should sleep on. I'm sure we will be very late though."

"I've managed many children through the years. I'll eat the remainder of caramel corn and get fat. I'll be happy as can be watching television; I adore movies also!"

"Thank you, bless you," Mia said bending down to kiss Maggie's cheek before they went out.

Angelo held the door for Mia at the rented car. "I'll need help with this navigation system!" he exclaimed.

She put in the address for St. James Cathedral, and they were on their way. "It's not too far, but I want plenty of time to find good parking and a seat close to the front of the church so we can see and hear more easily."

"Have you been to Mass there?"

"No, Papa. I haven't been to Mass in twenty years or more. I don't think I believe in Catholicism."

"Then why go to Mass?"

"I want to go with you—like when I was little."

"Especially tonight it will be a moving service."

Eyes gleaming, Mia nodded. "I miss the pageantry."

Light steamed from the windows of the cathedral as they approached.

"It's so beautiful," Mia sighed, glancing up at the majestic architecture. "The two towers soaring into the sky remind me of Mexican churches."

"Lovely."

Arched stained glass above the door showed Christ welcoming with simple words, "I am the vine, you are the branches."

They stepped through bronze doors covered in scenes of the journey of humanity to the heavenly city. Above the vestibule was a hundred year old organ with 51 ranks and over 3,000 pipes. Music was playing softly from it and another organ with 48 ranks—sets of pipes with similar timbre and volume.

Straight ahead of the entrance doors was a round font and a small pool. A wide center aisle led beyond to a square altar of white marble set on a circle of black slate in the physical center of the cathedral.

Once seated, Angelo and Mia took in the impressive features of stained glass windows and statues of saints illuminated by flickering candles and golden lights. Exquisite religious art spoke of elegance and faith. The Mass proceeded with colorful vestments and intricate movements like a kaleidoscope. Music from the organs and choir brought many to rapturous tears.

"I was transported," Mia whispered at the conclusion. "Did you feel *it*?"

"Feel what, Darling?"

"A vibrating presence hovering near."

Angelo smiled wistfully. "Sometimes I do feel that. Perhaps it's my Victoria."

"Oh, Papa, how ever did you get over her and fall for Maggie only a few months later?"

"I did *not* get over her. There's not been a day without her in my heart. But I live on, and I have a big heart. There is room enough for Maggie. Victoria did not want me to be alone. We talked of it many times. I know she is not alone. She's in the company of Our Heavenly Father and other loved ones."

Mia blinked back tears. "I miss Mother. Especially at Christmas. She always made it so perfectly gorgeous."

"She loved preparing for the holidays."

"I remember how magical it seemed. When I lived in Portland, I tried to make our store and home as beautiful as my memories. Somehow though, it never felt the same and I didn't know why. I began to think, if we had a baby, I could capture that magic," Mia sighed. "This year, finally, I have Peyton, and we had such special things planned."

"Plans are altered. Life intervenes."

"And death."

Angelo nodded with a tender look to her.

"I feel as if I'm walking in a strange dream."

"Time will help if not filled with too much activity. Tough to have quiet with a child in the house, though."

"Peyton wonders where his daddy is. It helps with you and Maggie here for distraction," she said as they pulled up to the house.

He leaned over and kissed her cheek. "Nowhere we would rather be."

Maggie was dozing on the sofa bed, but woke when they came inside.

They all went to the kitchen. Mia whipped up some eggs while Angelo grated cheese. She added sautéed onions and threw in some spinach before flipping the top of the eggs over.

"I'm not hungry, but that sure smells good," Maggie yawned. "I'll make toast."

"How did it go? Any sound from the baby?"

"I looked in several times. Just sleeping peacefully."

"That's my sweet boy. So easy."

"Were you an easy baby? You're so 'chill' now."

Mia's brow furrowed as she dished up the eggs. "Was I Papa?"

"No, Darling. You were several months old when we first met, but I remember your solemn face with large eyes staring and silent tears rolled down your little cheeks. It was many months before you smiled. I think that was at the holidays! You seemed to come alive with the twinkling lights, bright colors, and gleaming decorations."

"I swear I remember seeing my first Christmas tree! It had many sizes of bright blue balls frosted like snow."

"I believe that is correct. Every year Victoria filled the tree with new ornaments."

"That must be why there were so many boxes."

Angelo sighed, "It was a source of joy for her, and I must say, aggravation for me. I thought it excessive. But she had so few requirements and joys, I let her have what she wanted."

Smiling, Maggie leaned over and planted a kiss on his cheek. "You're a good husband. She broke you in well."

He chuckled.

"A good daddy, too." Mia looked up from her plate. "Peyton will need a stand in daddy when he gets older."

"My goodness! I haven't a clue what to do with a young boy! My father didn't either. He put me to work in his grocery as soon as I could hold a broom. It's all he knew. Work. I know many things now, but most were learned from books, not experience."

Mia was shaking her head. "You seem to be an expert on many subjects."

"I read extensively. Reading is pleasant respite from the hectic pace of business and life."

"You have a diverse book collection in the study."

"I've been thinking some books should come your way." He finished his last bite of toast. "Or all of them."

"Oh, Papa, I'd love them. But I don't know what I'd do with so many!"

"Perhaps I can donate some to a university."

"No, no! I want to read all the books first! I'll find somewhere for them," Mia yawned. "Let's leave the dishes until morning. You two take my bed. I changed the sheets earlier. I'll be quick asleep on the sofa bed."

"That is too kind," Maggie responded.

"Thank you, Darling. Good night."

Settling down in the living room, Mia retrieved Gerald's pillow from the closet and drifted to sleep breathing his scent.

It was dark. Gerald walked toward her.

Dim light began to shine on him,

illuminating only his face: brown eyes with

crinkles at the corners. He wore a suit of red.

Outstretched hands held a glistening white

camellia.

"Gerald," she whispered. "I'm so glad

you're here for Christmas!"

But when Mia's eyes opened, he was gone, and she wept silent tears onto his pillow.

Ants

Tiny bells jingled, faintly at first, then louder.

Mia tiptoed into Peyton's room and over to his crib. "Good morning, baby," she whispered.

He dropped the jingling stuffed toy and stood up.

She leaned in. Little arms wrapped around her neck. "It's your first Christmas little man," Mia said carrying him into the living room.

"OOOO," he cooed, pointing at the shining tree.

"Look! Something's in here!" She unhooked his stocking from the holder on the mantel and pulled out a doll made of coarse cotton. Appliquéd blue pants were hand stitched onto a reddish tan body. Satin stiches formed dark brown eyes and red lips on the face. Long strands of dark yarn were braided on each side of the head.

"Dada!"

"It's a boy. Like you when you're bigger," Mia smiled. "Daddy and I made it for you."

Peyton clutched the doll and struggled to be put down. Mia set him on the floor, and with gleaming eyes watched as he examined the figure closely.

Angelo and Maggie awoke and came out in robes and slippers.

"Merry Christmas," Mia chimed. "Coffee?"

"We could use it after another short night."

"I hope you slept okay."

"We did, Darling, We're glad to be up early to see the little man on his first Christmas morning," Angelo replied, kissing Mia on the cheek.

She made raisin-cinnamon toast and got out mugs for coffee. "Or I could make Mexican chocolate…"

"Victoria loved Mexican chocolate."

"I made some yesterday with a dash of cayenne. My stomach was upset all evening. Or, maybe it was the popcorn…"

Their eyes were soft on her face.

No cars were moving outside on the damp streets, and the three were eating and sipping in the quiet as they finished.

"We could plan supper," Maggie suggested.

But no ideas were proposed.

"Maybe too early to think about that. We could watch *Charlie Brown Christmas*?"

They settled in the living room with more coffee and the movie and played with Peyton. About ten o'clock, Maggie said, "Maybe this is a good time to phone Angelina."

"I'm ready," Mia answered, setting her phone on speaker and making the call. "Grandmother?"

"Mia, my darling. I'm glad to talk to you finally. My heart is crushed with your news."

"Thank you, Grandmother. I miss you," she replied with wavering voice.

"I am sorry to be infirmed and unable to be there."

"We wish you could be here," Maggie chimed in on the speaker phone.

"Thank you, dear. What is planned for supper?"

"We can't seem to decide," Maggie answered.

"We have your recipes from Mother…"

"I prefer soft, cheesy foods at times of high need."

"Lasagna?"

"Angelo's and my dear Federico's favorite."

"You make the BEST lasagna in the world, Grand-mother! My mouth is watering just thinking of it!"

"Thank you. You are very kind to this old woman."

Mia blinked back tears. "You're not so old!"

"I'm suddenly feeling my years. You must come with little Peyton for a visit soon."

"Yes," Mia nodded, motioning to Maggie to jump in on the conversation.

"Angelina, what should we make with the lasagna?"

"Do you have cabbage, capers, red wine vinegar?"

"Yes, Grandmother," Mia answered.

"Make my cabbage salad. And bread of course."

"Mother, you are filling our minds with delicious ideas!" Angelo chuckled.

"Keep light on the sausage so the little one can eat the lasagna."

"Okay, yes, we will," they replied in unison.

"Best get busy with the bread immediately. Takes a good time to rise. Don't rush it, right Mia? Treat it tender like a baby."

Mia laughed, "I will Grandmother. And I'll give the dough a pat like on a baby's behind for you."

"Good," Angelina said in pleasant tone. And then

she asked, "When is the service to be held?"

"It's a memorial. On the 27th at 2 P.M. at the school," Mia answered.

"This is acceptable to his family?"

"Gerald had no other family that I know of. His grandmother, Charlotte, passed last year. She raised him some years after his father died."

"Oh, my. How sad for him. And his mother?"

"She apparently deserted the family after his little brother, Henry, was killed in an accident outside their apartment. The boys had been playing in the dirt. When Gerald went inside for water, a neighbor backed his car out and ran over Henry."

Angelina gasped. "Unfathomable loss."

"Yes," they all sighed.

"What traditions of his culture do you follow?"

"We haven't followed any yet. Gerald's mother was not Native American. I actually don't know much of what he believed. But I've researched some. Native Americans believe life is a continuum extending beyond death of the body. The spirit first makes a journey over the places where the person has been on earth. After a service, and a meal, it is believed the spirit lingers a few more days around family and friends before departing on the next journey."

"How lovely. What of a burial?"

Mia struggled to answer, "He'll be cremated. I'm not sure what I will do with his ashes."

"OH?"

"He never said what would be his wishes. There," she swallowed hard, "wasn't time. We were busy making a life together."

"As it should be, Darling," Angelo commented.

"You will decide as is best," Angelina responded with warmth.

"I hope so."

"Thank you for the call, dear ones. Hugs and kisses to my grandson, Peyton."

"Merry Christmas, Grandmother."

"Merry Christmas, Mother Angelina," Maggie said.

"Best get on to cooking!"

"It's not as late here as there, Mother," Angelo laughed. "Did you attend morning Mass? Mia and I went last night while Maggie stayed with Peyton."

"It was quite lovely. Beatrice drove me over."

"Good. She is a faithful neighbor."

"Yes. I hope you have good neighbors, Mia. People nearby can lend a hand after family leaves."

"I probably do, Grandmother. Though it is not my

habit, or Gerald's, to reach out to them."

"A lesson to learn, my dear! Friends, even those known briefly, can be great comfort and assistance. Allow them to provide service to you. We are meant to accept grace of God, and man."

"Thank you, Grandmother. I'll try."

"Victoria, bless her soul, found it nearly impossible to learn that lesson. Thankfully though, she allowed *me* to share some things with the family."

"Yes, Mother. Your guidance and assistance has meant the world to us," Angelo offered.

"Thank you, son. You are a good man, a good husband," Angelina replied. And she added with a hint of stern humor, "Good *women* have greatly influenced you."

"*You* are a strong woman, Grandmother."

"I am blessed beyond measure," Angelina replied with a crack in her voice. "I am thankful for all of you and for this call on Christmas. Now go make your bread!"

They did as Angelina instructed: made the bread, a pan of lasagna and the salad. And it was all perfect.

Angelo and Maggie returned to their hotel early, and Mia went to bed shortly after Peyton. She slept long and hard without dreams to remember.

But in the morning, she woke with a start, jumped

out of bed and checked her phone, "Oh, no." She dressed quickly and got Peyton up and changed and fed and strapped into his car seat. Then they sped down the road.

Her phone rang. She answered on speaker, and said, "I'm almost there, Mama."

Rosalia, Benito, and Marisol were standing on the curb outside Arrivals at SeaTac airport when she drove up. Mia unlatched the trunk and jumped out. She hugged each one, helped load the luggage, and they all got into the car.

"Peyton so big now!" Marisol oozed.

Benito played with the baby's hand and giggled.

"*My* baby look tired," Rosalia said reaching over and lightly stroking Mia's cheek.

"I am, Mama. But thank goodness I woke before you had been standing forever! Sorry you had to wait."

Rosalia shook her head and smiled, "Watch cars, trucks, people. So different from Mexico."

Relief showed on her face. Mia glanced in the rear-view mirror at the children. "Good to see you all! Did you have a good Christmas?"

"Best part *now*: see Mama Mia."

"You're my great gifts! Have you eaten? Do they feed you on the red-eye flight?"

"Enough for now. We eat more later," Rosalia said.

"Okay, good."

They arrived at Seattle Children's Hospital with a few minutes to admire the giant murals of wildlife they'd so enjoyed on previous visits.

"This place make happy heart," Rosalia commented with a smile. "Healing, too, I think!"

"Like this," Benito pointed at a turtle.

"I like bears!" Marisol said.

"No, this!" Benito grinned pointing at an insect.

"I don't like bugs!" she squealed. "I like otters!"

"Okay, okay," Mia laughed. "We can like them all!"

The children were laughing and chattering when arriving at the check-in desk.

A nurse they met last year greeted them, "My goodness! Our man, Benito! Look how tall you have grown! And what a handsome smile you now have!"

He giggled and grinned.

"Bet your check-up will go swimmingly!"

Though he'd learned a great deal of English already, he did not understand and only shrugged.

"Good-luck. *Buena suerte!*" the nurse offered.

Marisol and Benito both smiled at her attempt to speak Spanish.

"*Muchas gracias*," Rosalia replied with appreciative

nod to the nurse before they went on down the hall.

Several doctors examined Benito and discussed with Mia options for future surgeries if needed as his face grew.

"The scars of the cleft lip are fading and the cleft palette has healed quite well. All in all, an excellent result!" Dr. Vincent Andrew (*Dr. Andy*) Rayburn said.

"Thank you so much for your kind expertise," Mia replied. "And thank you for your assistance in helping us line up the medical care he needed when in Mexico."

"Have the children come to live in the U.S. now?"

"They live with an aunt and cousins in Oaxaca and only just arrived. Scheduling an appointment on a Saturday around the holidays was a blessing. We're so thankful..." Mia's eyes pooled with tears.

"Glad we could help! Who is this little one?" Dr. Andy asked easily while smiling at the baby in Mia's arms.

"My son, Peyton. He'll be one year old soon."

"Best wishes to you all! Hope to see you again," Dr. Andy said shaking their hands.

"Can we go home now?" Marisol asked hopping and sidestepping down the hall and pulling Benito along. "I want to see Kelsey! Can they come over?"

"Ummm, I'll have to see what their plans are," Mia said checking her phone. "After twelve already."

"Can she stay over? We can sleep on the floor and Mama Rosalia can sleep on the sofa bed with Benito?" Marisol pleaded.

"Your enthusiasm is welcome!" Mia laughed.

Rosalia nodded, pride showing on her face while watching. "Learn much each day out of aunt's house."

"Maybe the learning center *will be* very helpful," Mia conceded as they loaded into the car.

Traffic was not heavy considering it was a weekend and the day after Christmas when shoppers were out in droves. But Peyton began yowling and the trip to the house was difficult despite the children's efforts to placate him.

They shuttled all the suitcases and diaper bag and baby into the house.

"Whew! I'm so glad that's all finished," Mia said.

"Nana Lia make food. Daughter take care of baby."

"That would be wonderful, Mama. Thank you. Kids: wash hands, and help set the table for lunch."

"Only four plus baby?"

Nodding, Mia said, "Yes, I don't know when Papa and Maggie will be over." After changing his diaper, Mia put Peyton in his high chair, and heated soft sweet potato and green beans. He gobbled down bite after bite as fast as she could spoon it to him.

"Let me try!" Marisol begged. "Please!"

Mia handed over the spoon, but Peyton turned his head away each time Marisol brought it near.

"Baby think only Mama feed," Rosalia observed. "This week Peyton learn different also good!"

Mia flashed a look as if wounded, but accepted the spoon back from Marisol and continued feeding.

Rosalia and the children ate chicken *quesadillas* (tortillas with chicken and cheese), and sliced bananas. Benito offered a large piece to Peyton who grabbed it, stuffed the banana in his mouth, and grinned.

"See eat!"

"Good. He can have more if you want to share."

The children eagerly gave Peyton chunks of banana and laughed at his impish grins and gobbling.

Finally he made it clear he was done by holding a bite over the edge of his tray and threatening to drop it to the floor. "Okay, okay. That's all," Mia said wiping his face and hands, and set him down.

"No eat? Daughter need keep strength."

She shook her head. "I'm not hungry. I'll have something after a bit."

While Rosalia cleared up the kitchen and the children played with Peyton's toys, Mia went into the bedroom.

She sat down on the bed. Her hand stroked the soft old quilt with colors of red, yellow, and blue on the background of night. Her fingers traced a swirl around and around and her head grew heavy. She stretched out on her side and closed her eyes.

An hour passed before Mia woke with a start and staggered to Peyton's room. Finding him asleep in his crib, she reached down and stroked his chubby cheek and thick dark hair.

"We made a beautiful boy," she whispered as if Gerald was there. "I know you're not far away, but I wish I could hold you, feel your arms around me."

Rosalia quietly came into the room and took Mia's hand, leading her out and shutting the door.

"Thank you for putting him down for nap, Mama."

They scrunched onto the sofa beside Marisol and Benito watching the *Charlie Brown Christmas* movie.

"I almost forgot!" Mia made a call on her phone.

Deena answered right away. "How are you doing?" Can I help with anything for tomorrow?"

"We're okay. Actually, yes. I need to make displays for the memorial. I know from your real estate brochures, you have a good eye for arrangement and description."

"Will you mount pictures? I have several dry erase

boards you could use. They'd be good with easels or to hold up and show by hand. They're stiff so it'll be easy to remove the pictures later."

"I have only a handful of photos of Gerald, but I have pictures of murals he painted and other photographs he took. His principal at Adams Elementary said she might have a few photographs of him with students and teachers, but I won't get those until tomorrow."

"Should I come over today about four o'clock?"

"Thank you, yes," Mia exhaled. "Marisol is here! She wonders if Kelsey can stay the night?"

"Sure if you're up to it. I can pick her up before the service."

"I think it will be fine for me. Fun for the children and a good distraction while the adults work."

"Sounds good. See you in a while."

Mia thanked her, then called Joyce. "I'm pulling together plans for the service. Did you reach your friend?"

"Yes, and he's glad to do it. He'll be there at one o'clock to get a copy of what you want him to read."

"Great, thank you. Deena's coming over today at four o'clock to help organize the displays of photographs. Would you like to come, too? Bring Susan if she wants. We'll make something for supper..."

"I can bring macaroni and cheese, French bread, chicken fingers, kale salad."

"That'd be fantastic. Thank you, Joyce. You're so sweet to me."

"You're my friend. My heart hurts now, too."

Wiping away tears, Mia said, "Just get over here. I could use one of your hugs."

"Be there four-ish."

After Peyton's nap and snack, the children played. Mia fixed a cup of chamomile tea, and sat at the table with paper and pen.

Death is not an ending

Love lives on

through every act and kindness

Deena, Kelsey, and Joyce arrived. The children laughed and talked excitedly. Snacks were put out, and the friends worked on displays while Rosalia tended Peyton.

"I didn't know Gerald was such an accomplished artist," Deena said looking at the pictures. "His murals are intriguing. They remind me of an impressionist's paintings, I forget which one. But the use of light is beautiful."

Mia nodded. "Yes, surprising. Many layers…"

"Like an onion with layer upon layer."

Mia sighed, "He didn't boast, or talk much about what was on his mind. I think I could spend a lifetime knowing him and would still be surprised by what I didn't know about him."

"A complex man."

"I'm glad he was such a good one," Deena said. "We're all glad he came into your life, and ours. He helped restore more my faith in men, and in the wonder of life—how it unfolds hidden mysteries."

Mia nodded, dabbing at her eyes. "Yes," she breathed.

Cranes

The coffee maker gasped and sputtered dark coffee dripping like tears. It might have been a replay from the past—another house, another husband, another aching loss.

But Mia did not linger in the bed or hide her head this time. She hurried to the kitchen, poured a big mug of coffee, and doctored the brew to white and sweet. Her hands shook. She leaned against the counter and drank.

After showering and braiding her hair, she slipped on her red dress—the one worn on Martin Luther King Day last year for their wedding at Golden Gardens Park with the mountains, water, and sky as witness. But no matter how much sentiment might linger in the fabric, the softly pleated dress from pregnancy would be too warm worn under a coat indoors to hide its volume. And questions about the possible "meaning" of wearing such a 'big' dress would be intolerable. The black dress with lace worn on Christmas was too fancy for daytime. "Pants?" She slid hangers along the rod—business styles from her 'past life' in Portland when childless and soon to be divorced. She had ached and cried back then. But somehow now, there was a sense of calm in her actions. She chose a Rayon shift dress with simple round neck and long, straight sleeves. The pattern of greens suggested leaves. After rummaging through a drawer, she found the ribbons they'd worn on their wedding day in the park. Mia tied them around her neck and jingled the bells on the ends. She smiled with a lump in her throat, but no tears came.

After everyone was up and fed and dressed, and Peyton had finished a short morning nap, Joyce and Deena arrived. They carted out the displays and diaper bag and vase of white camellias from the bush Gerald had given Mia. She loaded Peyton in her car while the others got in theirs, and the caravan began.

Adams Elementary was not far. Mia parked and glanced up at the mosaic sign of snow capped mountains, trees, eagles, bumblebees, deer, coyotes, blue sky, water, and plants. Beauty. Nature. Life. Branches from knobby sycamores hung overhead. Mia as a child would have wrapped her arms around the massive trunks of the trees. Her hands would have brushed over the greying bark. Her fingers would have searched the ground for fallen leaves to pocket. No time now. A car full of children and her mother were waiting to go inside.

They made their way up to the school, their eyes on the old bricks and windows and roof, a huge mural of an octopus, and owl, and a Billy goat climbing a mountain.

"I like this school!" Marisol said.

Benito pointed and squealed and smiled agreement.

Inside, the children gawked and oooed and ahhhed at art posted on the walls—paintings and paper murals of nature. Origami cranes of every color and size suspended on strings hovered overhead.

"Why all these?"

"There's a story Gerald told me from Japan. It is said if one folds 1000 origami cranes, a wish will be granted."

"What wish?"

"I don't know," Mia sighed.

"I have wish," Marisol said loudly. "I wish Gerald here."

Mia blinked. "He *is* here. We just can't see him in

the flesh."

"I like his big hugs."

"Me, too sweetie. Me, too."

They found seats in the cafeteria. Mia and her helpers set up the displays. People filed in. The principal lavished condolences on Mia and family.

Joyce's friend came over and introduced himself, "I'm Westin Prince."

Mia stared and offered her hand.

Joyce intervened. "Westin has been volunteering where Susan works. I like his commanding voice. I thought his presence would be comforting."

"Yes," Mia managed to say.

"I'll go over what it is you have prepared," he said.

"OH. Yes." Mia fumbled in her bag for the handwritten piece, and gave the rumpled paper to him.

"Thank you. I'll need a few minutes of quiet." He walked toward the hallway.

Locking eyes with Joyce—who smiled and shrugged—Mia said in a whisper, "Something you forgot to mention."

"I didn't forget. Thought it better not to mention."

"I see."

"He's perfect for the task in every way. And he was

quite generous in agreeing to come."

Mia glanced again toward the hallway and pushed down rising tension with a hand to her neck.

Benches and chairs filled. The crowd hushed as the principal stepped up to the microphone. She introduced Mia, who introduced family and friends sitting in a semicircle of chairs beside her.

The principal addressed the assembled crowd, "Thank you for taking time from your holiday celebrations to join us in honoring a wonderful man. Most of us met Gerald only one year ago. But this talented teacher quickly endeared himself to students and teachers alike. He had great enthusiasm for art. But it was not the racing heart and quick moving kind of enthusiasm. Gerald demonstrated quiet confidence and competence. His knowledge was conveyed in an almost osmotic fashion. We were amazed by how quickly our students began producing first rate art. What he has begun here, we will continue. He opened all our eyes to many great gifts we share. He influenced other staff and parents who will now take up the gauntlet in bringing Adams Elementary philosophy and creativity to the world."

The crowd remained hushed.

Mia stepped up. "I had Gerald as husband for less

than a year. But in that time, he was everything and more than I could want. He had a special way about him. He shared many gifts. He will be forever in my heart." Her eyes teared up, her voice caught in her throat.

"May I present my friend, Westin Prince," Joyce said relieving Mia at the microphone. "Westin has a few words."

The extremely fit, amber skinned man with grey and flowing hair stepped up. "Thank you. I am honored to say a few words about a man I did not have the pleasure of knowing. I hail from Canada. I am First American. Gerald was Native American."

Joyce held up a photo of Gerald tending plants in a garden.

Westin continued addressing the murmuring assemblage. "Gerald's father's family were of the Wy'am people who inhabited an extensive area of influence and trade along the Columbia River for thousands of years. Salmon forms the basis for the people's livelihood, customs, and very spirit. When the peoples were displaced, their ancient fishing grounds swallowed up by the swelling waters behind hydroelectric dams, many lost their connection to the land and traditions. They struggled to integrate into surrounding communities, a difficulty still experienced today. There is much mistrust and stereotyping on both sides of this complex issue of power and politics.

"Gerald's mother's family did not acknowledge the birth of Gerald or his younger brother, who succumbed in a tragic accident at the age of six. His mother deserted the family. His father passed away when Gerald was still a boy. He was then raised by his paternal grandmother, Charlotte, in The Dalles, Oregon, a small town along the Columbia. These influences of loss and culture and conflict show up in Gerald's intriguing art."

Deena held up a white board with the attached photo of the mural Gerald had painted of a woman's face obscured by water—Mia had once suggested Rufus, the tiny town where the mural was painted on an old shed, would be put on the world map of art. As if struck by the beauty of this image, the crowd sighed.

"Some wonder if this captivating woman is the spirit of the Wy'am peoples, or of the falls. Some wonder if this woman weeps for their many losses and is drowning in the tears of their sorrow," Prince said.

Heads nodded.

"Gerald loved history. He enjoyed gardening and growing his own food. He believed in learning. He believed in allowing others their own ideas. He said we should,

'Listen to what speaks.'"

Students smiled as if having heard the words before.

"Art is the eruption of deeply held talents and beliefs. It is the physical expression of grace."

Joyce and Deena held up more boards with photos of Gerald's paintings.

"I present again Gerald's wife, Mia, and his son, Peyton."

The room silenced.

Holding the baby in her arms, Mia stepped forward. She cleared her throat. "Gerald, went quickly, as quickly and quietly as he came into my life. Our time together as a couple, and as a family was short. His time teaching was also short." She shook her head, paused. "Many have kindly told me Gerald impressed them with his quiet strength, and his unique ability to communicate more than what he said. He was endlessly hopeful. He had a powerful mind. Encounters with that kind of creative spirit leave a mark. We are changed. Deeply marked and changed."

The crowd murmured.

"I was changed by knowing him. After meeting Gerald, I wrote my first novel. I will keep writing. It is part of me now. As much as he is part of me. I miss his presence beside me. But I feel him with me. I will go forward. I will keep on living, creating, re-creating." Mia paused, then chuckled, "Maybe you've heard Gerald say he believed in recycling, reusing, reinventing. He believed we are constantly being made and re-made through our experiences. Our thoughts, efforts, talents, and tribulations shape our present, form our future we could not have imagined without allowing beauty and light into our lives. When we allow spirit to move through us, we embody the creative power of life and the expression of love. Gerald would want you to move forward with your dreams. Don't look back. His inspiration lives and breathes through your creativity."

Joyce and Deena each held up a whiteboard with photos.

Mia did not look at the pictures of Gerald smiling: his dark brown eyes radiating warmth, his long, dark hair in a single braid down his back.

But pointing at the photos, Peyton said loudly, "Dada!"

Tears fled from many eyes.

A reception was held at the large and beautifully remodeled home of Lonni, Stephanie, and Deena. Though Mia was accompanied this time by family, friends, and Peyton, her heart pounded as she stepped through the door—other visits she had been here with Gerald.

Ira approached her, "Hi, Mia. How are you doing?"

"Okay," she smiled. "Thank you for the article. It presented Gerald in such positive light. I fell in love with him all over again."

Ira glanced at the floor. "Mostly your words. He was a good guy. Deena and I looked forward to spending time with you both in the future."

"Thank you," she replied. "That's very sweet."

He turned, his eyes scanning the room.

Deena noticed and excused herself from conversation with Lonni. She came over, kissed Ira, hugged Mia, greeted Peyton. "Hi, little buddy! Kelsey has been waiting to play with you!"

He squealed and smiled at Kelsey, Marisol, and Benito coming over.

"Come play with us! We have another big red ball!" Kelsey and Marisol took his hands, and Benito followed to an adjoining room. Sounds of the ball being rolled and bounced and their laughter echoed across the wood floors.

Mia smiled. "They're good together."

"Yes!" Deena chimed. "They were so well behaved last night at your house watching a movie, eating caramel corn with few fights or complaints! Kids are such a joy."

Ira gave her a look heavy with affection. His hand caressed the small of Deena's back and she sighed with obvious pleasure.

"Hmmm, something's heating up between you two."

They only smiled.

"Maybe one day Kelsey will have a sibling to play with?" she suggested.

"See what time brings," Ira said, but his look was neither evasive or unsure.

"Don't wait too long! You never know what might happen while you're waiting for all the right things to fall into place!" Her eyes pooled with tears. "I'm sorry. I…"

Angelo and Maggie joined them and encouraged Mia to eat.

"I don't need food."

"Darling, you could have salad. Just something."

"My body is as heavy as my heart," she complained. "I ate for the baby, ate for feeding the baby, ate in married contentment and comfort. I gained love and I gained pounds, but Gerald said I was beautiful no matter what."

"Of course you are."

"Papa," Mia's voice shook. "Now it's changed…"

"Come," Maggie offered an arm. "Let's have a drink."

Mia went and had a hot spiced cider. They talked of the service with other guests—teacher and administrator friends from the school, a few parents— who came over to give their condolences.

"Thank you, all. You're very kind. I…I'm touched. I remember when Mother passed, I was not comforted by well wishes. I felt lost. I couldn't let love in. But somehow, that changed."

They nodded, returned her smile.

The next days were busy with enriching activities for the children: visiting the Seattle Children's Museum, shopping center and café and restaurant play areas, Washington Park Arboretum and the Japanese Garden.

They all dropped into bed early each night, and Mia slept hard.

Ballistic

His long hair brushed across her chest.
He was smiling above her, shoulders
supported by muscular arms, chest bare.
They came together.
Her hands gripped his back.

"Ohhh," she sighed, tears rushing her
cheeks, a smile on her lips. "Ger…"
He looked at her, his eyes filled with love.
And then his face softened, grew hazy
and distant.

When Mia opened her eyes, Gerald was not there.

"You've left me," she whispered, going to the window and peering at the night sky. "Full moon coming. The end of our only year..."

She pulled on a robe and was sipping strong coffee white and sweet when everyone else woke.

Rosalia began making breakfast. "I 'International,' make French toast!"

Laughing, Mia, gave a kiss to her cheek. "You are a worldly woman!"

"Teach me to make this?" Marisol asked. "I want to be international cook! Mama Rosalia good teacher. Teach more people at big center!"

"Yes, I think Mama will be an awesome teacher."

Rosalia glanced at Mia. "Mama think this house too small and quiet."

"It will be terribly empty when you all go."

"Maybe daughter come, too."

"I couldn't possibly go. I have things to finish...all the details..." She shook her head, unable to say more, forced a smile. "Besides, I can't leave the house in winter; it's old and needs care, especially in rainy weather. A leak might develop, or the power could go out and everything would start getting mildewed and moldy."

Rosalia only shrugged.

Benito and Marisol finished setting the table.

"Why so many place settings?" Mia asked.

"Joyce and daughter come."

"Oh. Good." Mia rummaged through the cupboards for topping ingredients. She sifted powdered sugar and cinnamon with cocoa mix and put it in a sprinkle jar. Maple syrup was warmed. Juice poured. Vanilla ice cream was set out. Frozen strawberries were warmed.

"Much sweet for breakfast!" Marisol giggled.

Mia only smiled while cracking eggs.

"It's morning!" Joyce and Susan chimed as Marisol opened the door and they rushed in. They hugged her, and rambunctiously picked up Benito and Peyton, swung them around, and set them down.

Joyce looked at each person, and then said dramatically, "I have an announcement! I may be moving to Seattle to go to nursing school!"

"When?"

"Hopefully by the end of summer. I still need to be accepted into one of several programs I've applied to, but I have a good chance! And a back up plan."

"How exciting!"

"Yes! But I'm terrified to be studying alongside

'children' who could be my own!'"

Mia laughed. "You'll teach them something!"

"I'll be so proud of you, Mom," Susan said while bringing items to the table.

"Aren't you already?" Joyce quipped giving her a loving pat on the shoulder.

"Yes, of course, but it will be another great accomplishment for you," Susan countered.

"You mean a woman of my age?" Joyce grinned.

"What brought this on? It hasn't been long since you got your degree in social work. And you're already working in the field, sort of."

"I do like my job working with seniors. But I miss school. I love *learning* to do things much more than *actually* doing them."

"Not me. I love doing." Mia stated.

"Mama Rosalia move for make school!" Marisol interjected.

"Oh, my goodness. Where?"

"Mama is moving back to her hometown of San Bartolome Quialana to *start* a community school."

"What an undertaking! That will be a ton of work won't it?" Susan asked.

Rosalia nodded. "Mother need daughter help."

"Oh, that is a good idea!" Joyce said, but her smile faded seeing Mia shaking her head. "What *will* you do with yourself after they have gone? Just you and Peyton in a quiet house…"

Glancing around at the eyes on her, Mia said, "I'll figure ways to promote *Mending Stone,* and I'll start writing something new."

"Non-fiction? It would be awesome to read about how you found Rosalia, how Gerald found you twice!"

"Three times," Mia said quietly. "And again last night, with the full moon energy coming…" Her face heated. She turned to the sink, ran water over her hands and wiped them slowly dry before continuing. "I felt Gerald with me. And then, I was in the deepest void as if at the edge of the cliff, alone again. His spirit left."

Joyce's eyes teared up.

Rosalia watched with a face of concern.

"We eat?" Benito asked climbing into a chair.

Rosalia nodded, piled pieces of French toast onto a plate.

Mia placed Peyton in his high chair and fixed a piece of toast with a little syrup for him. She started to sit down, but then went to the cupboard and brought out a bottle of champagne. "Any one for Mimosa?"

Joyce and Susan and Rosalia thrust out glasses of orange juice. Mia popped the top, and poured.

"Me, too?" Marisol asked.

"A trickle!"

Marisol took a sip and giggled. "Sweet bubbles."

"Bubbles for me!" Benito demanded.

Mia gave him the last drizzle.

"Empty? You didn't get any," Susan said.

"I wanted you all to have it." Mia blinked back tears, and smiled, "We bought it to share on our anniversary. I'll have sweet sugar and fat on my French toast."

"I'll have that, too!" Joyce chuckled.

"Thank you for cooking, Mama," Mia said sprinkling the cocoa-cinnamon-sugar mixture over her buttered French toast.

"Eggs good! How so light and fluffy?"

"I whisked a bit of milk in."

"You could teach cooking!"

"Teach? I've never considered it," Mia shrugged.

"Do you have a college degree?" Susan inquired.

"No, I quit a few terms short. I'd been working part-time but gradually work took over. I had started dating Tim. I like bursts of learning, especially skill building, so I was excited for the opportunity to move to Portland and start our store. There was so much to learn and do with establishing the business."

"Sounds like you're a kinesthetic learner: learning by physical experience," Susan offered.

"I'm a 'reading and writing' kind of learner," Joyce said. "I like visuals. *Love* books, manuals…"

"I *like* books," Mia explained. "And I like knowing what's in them, but I'm more excited by hands on trials and errors."

"They say there are four main types of learners," Susan elaborated. "Visual, auditory, kinesthetic, and reading/writing."

Lively talk about education continued around the table. After everyone finished eating, the children settled down in front of the television to watch a parade Mia had taped. Even Peyton was entranced by the colorful costumes, floats, and music.

"They're so cute together," Joyce observed.

Nodding, Mia responded, "Peyton is changing every day. It's been good for him to be with the other children. Not sure what we'll do with just two of us…"

"When it gets quiet, don't run from your grief. Do the work."

"What work?"

"Letting yourself *feel*."

"Gerald used to say that, too," Mia sighed.

"A wise man."

"He had a way of knowing what I need before I even know it myself."

"You were blessed to find each other. Don't forget: work through the stages. Take as long as you need."

Mia nodded, and whispered, "I will."

Later, the guests departed. Marisol and Benito went for the night with Deena and Kelsey and some other young friends. Peyton was down. Even Rosalia settled on the sofa, enthralled with a soap opera in Spanish.

Mia went to her room. She opened the closet filled to capacity with her clothes, shoes, sweaters, purses, Gerald's clothes, and shoes neatly lined up beside a cardboard box given to her by the school principal. She stared down at it as if something startling might jump out.

She carried the box over to the bed, and dislodged the lid. Inside were items from Gerald's desk at school. She removed pens and pencils, a ruler. Dictionary. Scissors. A sketch book. Scrap paper. Paint brushes, water color paints, a small tray with dried pigments settled into the depressions. Beneath all these, were photographs printed on cut

3x5 inch papers. She rifled through the stack, studied the last one, returned to the first.

"What was he planning to do with this?" She studied them again. Two holes were pierced through one end of each page as if for binding together. She looked again into the box. A piece of supple leather and a thin strip like a lace lay in the bottom.

"Ohhh," she sighed, eyes pooling. "Making a book." Mia counted the pages. "Fifty-two. Fifty-two weeks in a year?" Faintly penciled words lined the bottoms of some of the pages. "Wise words, instructive calls to action—as if for therapy. Gerald," she whispered, hands shaking. "What did you mean to do with this? Did you know? Did you know I would need your words and images?"

Fury colored her cheeks.

"Did you *know* something was wrong?"

Ballistic grief gripped her.

She was shaking, clutching her chest.

Hot tears poured down.

She collapsed on the bed. Her hands gripped the old quilt and pushed and pulled as if in a fight. But it ended as suddenly as it began.

Mia sat up and looked again at the pictures, slowly this time, letting the colors and subjects and words have their way with her. And calm reigned.

> My love fell down
>
> down down
>
> in a well of grief
>
> Down it sank in dank and dark and cold
>
> and lingered there
>
> But sun overhead gleamed on the water
>
> And with surface warming
>
> ripples rose

Mia scribbled words on a blank sheet of paper: old lines she'd written long ago.

> Fire under water burns
>
> red beneath the blue
>
> Neither fades nor flares
>
> with passing time
>
> nor dreams begun anew

She sighed, "So much passion." Her finger traced the swirling stitches on the quilt and more words flowed into her mind.

My love
come down
Come round the stone
Rest easy
heart like grass waving in wind

Tears streamed her face. "Will I ever feel that again? Why did you do this? Why did you leave me?"

Her face a mask of sorrow, she thumbed through the images again: Gerald's photographs produced to look like paintings. Achingly beautiful. Wistful.

"We were building a family…We were busy, but I thought we had time," she cried. "We were settling into a future of comfort," Mia pounded the bed with her fist. "Again? Again I have to learn this? Comfort is a LIE!'"

My love fell down
Down down in a well of grief
My love is lost
drowning in waves of tears
Nothing makes sense
I have family but they cant touch my need

Not like you

Not the way you eased me into life

and made me feel safe

with only the sound of your breath

and the feel of your skin

Next morning, she was up, and went out to the other room. "Mama? Are you awake?"

Rosalia roused and patted the couch bed beside her.

Mia sat down, rested her head on her mother's soft chest. She closed her eyes. "Thank you for being here. Thank you for loving me so much."

"Easy. Mother shares heart with child."

"Did you ever wish for more children?"

Rosalia nodded, "Wish this when young, before so much happen, before Guillermo…"

"Oh, Mama," Mia whispered.

"How I ached to hold daughter. Ached for Mano. Ached for family left behind. And babies no have."

"When I was with Tim. I thought what we had was good. I tried not to ache for something more. But I did want more. SO much more! After losing so many chances for a baby, I thought I would break. And when Tim strayed to Valerie, I thought my life was over. But it was only changing—the past was gone and the future hadn't arrived. The days felt empty and pointless. But the weeks along the Columbia with Gerald were like languishing in care. I was restored. I had courage to face what I'd avoided too long—facing Mother and Papa with the truth: I'd lost myself in striving too hard for financial gain, lost faith and hope and courage."

Rosalia patted her own chest. "This *I* feel, also!"

"Yes! That's why it was so easy to write the story of *Mending Stone*—the emotion of Rosa was as real as my own! And now..." Mia whispered. "I've lost my beloved like you lost my father, Mano. I don't know how you went on. Or how I will."

Rosalia nodded, wiping away tears. "But daughter have Peyton. And Marisol and Benito."

"It's so expensive with children. I just don't see a way to move forward. I won't have Gerald's salary for bills and I don't want to put Peyton in day care! That's not what we wanted for him. Gerald and I the future all planned..."

Rosalia gently patted Mia's shoulder, and replied quietly, "Life has plan."

"But what now?" she asked in barely audible tone.

Rosalia said gently, "Have family for some help."

Mia sighed. "It is emotional comfort. I did have only

acquaintances in Portland. But here I have Deena and other friends. Joyce may be moving here. And Gerald, apparently, made many friends at school. Though *I* don't know them, perhaps I will eventually. And once Peyton starts school, I will meet other parents."

"Make friends in village: help plan school for San Bartolome Quialana!"

Mia responded with reservation, "I didn't major in education, but I did learn some this year with Gerald's lesson planning."

"Mama need help make space."

"You mean the classroom designs?"

Rosalia nodded.

"Will Javier design the school building?"

"No, no! Find architect. Javier build. Need ideas!"

"I *am* good with ideas. I've enjoyed writing—something I never expected to do for money, but I *really* love creative problem solving."

Her mother nodded.

"It'd be hard to help you with limited phone service in San Bartolome Quialana, though. How could we exchange information?"

Rosalia shrugged, smiled. "*Ojalla.*"

"What did you say?"

"God willing. *Si Dios quiere todas las cosas*: God willing all things."

"Yeess," Mia answered as Peyton began calling and she got up and headed toward his room. "I need to remember that."

"Remember pray! *La Virgen de Guadalupe* listen. Mother's heart have answers."

"Answers to what questions? You're speaking in riddles, Mama," Mia exclaimed from the other room while changing Peyton's diaper.

"Time for go now."

"OH! I nearly forgot it's today! Oh, no! I'm not ready, and little man needs a bath. I'll hurry. Then we can get Marisol and Benito."

"Nana Lia dress baby. Daughter dress self."

Mia laughed. "You're bossy, Mama."

Laughing also, Rosalia responded, "Javier say this! *I* say woman strong, tell man how make good life!"

"Oh, my gosh! That sounds like something Grandmother Angelina says! You're two peas in a pod," Mia said running a brush through her hair. They loaded the luggage into the car, picked up the children, headed for the airport. There was little time for good-byes: hugs and declarations of love and then off they went waving.

Mia was in tears by the time she pulled out onto the freeway. Peyton fell asleep. Unwilling to wake him, she kept driving and barely noticed where she was until her car drove into the line at Mukelteo ferry. Cars eased forward with clunks of wheels on heavy planks and steel. She parked, slid down in her seat, and closed her eyes while the ferry moved across Puget Sound.

Words fell between them.
Sweet claims.
She cried, "What can I do now?"
He shrugged.
"Why don't you tell me what to do?"
He only smiled slowly in his gentle way, his eyes dark brown, warming. "I want you…"
"Want me? *How*? How can I have you? I can't touch you. I can barely feel you…"
He only shrugged, turned and walked away
with easy movement of his hips and shoulders
going out the door.

She woke to the sound of cars rolling off the ferry one by one at Clinton. Stair stepping across the south end of Whidbey Island, Mia drove to Dave Mackie Public Park. A light drizzle was coming down. "I brought Marisol to this island last year. So much I didn't know yet," Mia sighed. "So much was about to change, and now it's all undone."

Tears fell in warm splotches on her arms.

"Mother Mary, why did you let me fall so hard for Gerald if he was to be lost? We planned such wonderful times ahead! And now I'm left alone with Peyton."

Her hands gripped the steering wheel.

Wind buffeted the car. A swing at the playground moved and squeaked on rusty links.

She watched attentively.

A crumpled paper fluttered across the grass. A large bird swooped down as if to snatch it, but gave up and circled the park, flying closer and swooping toward her car.

"I get it. I'm not alone."

Peyton stirred.

"Little man, are you waking?" Mia smiled in the rear-view mirror at his face reflected by a mirror mounted to the back seat. He grinned.

She got out, unstrapped and changed him, then walked with him wrapped in her arms over to the swing. She sat down. The thick rubber seat clung to her hips. Her feet pushed off. "Wheee!"

Peyton giggled.

Several children ran up, threw themselves down on their bellies in swings, and pushed off. The swings creaked and moaned back and forth, back and forth. One boy turned to sit and pumped his legs hard, powering the swing. After reaching maximum height, the boy leapt out of the swing, hit the ground, and was off running fast.

"Don't get any ideas!" Mia instructed Peyton with a smile as he squirmed in her arms. "No dangerous jumping! We can't take the risk you'll..." But she shivered, and couldn't finish what she might have said.

They went back to the car and drove across the island toward Langley, stopped at a restaurant.

Neil's Clover Patch Café sported cheerful green letters above the door and a red neon 'open' sign. Inside, Mia set Peyton down on the high backed vinyl booth. The waiter brought a baby seat, and took her order for grilled cheese and cream of chicken soup. She entertained Peyton with dramatic opening of multiple cellophane packages of soda crackers and tried to feed him, but he refused every bite.

"Cute," a passing woman commented. "Grandson?"

Mia looked up, shock on her face, and found no response other than a pained smile. As the woman walked away, she shook her head and muttered to herself, "Grandson! I should be so lucky! Maybe twenty-five years from now!"

They shared bites of the grilled cheese sandwich, but Peyton refused to be fed the soup. She handed him the spoon and he dug in. "Little man, you're growing up. Pretty soon I will call you my BIG man!"

He grinned with mouth full.

After cleaning him up in the rest room, they went out to the car, and she drove one direction, then another. On a corner of main street in Langley, she paused outside the Saratoga Inn. Shingled cedar siding and white wrap-around porches invited travelers to linger and take in the water views, especially from second-story rooms with balconies. If she was considering staying the night, the thought was eliminated by sudden loud outbursts from the baby in the back seat.

Mia resumed driving, but slow enough to get a glimpse of water views she'd shared with Marisol on their visit last year while Benito was hospitalized. She glanced down a street for a quick view of the Langley Clock Shop where they'd purchased the sale item for him: an owl clock.

Time.

Mia was on a tight budget back then, just like now.

Sun was dropping low by the time they reached the ferry. Mia sang little songs to amuse Peyton during the crossing. Once landed, heading south on the freeway through Seattle, she phoned Joyce. "What are your plans tomorrow? Want to come over to make cookies like we did at your house two years ago?"

"How many kinds?"

"Six each might be a few too many to make with a baby underfoot!" Mia laughed.

"Have Grandmother Angelina's favorite recipes?"

"Of course."

"Tell me we don't have to eat them all! I'm giving up my hips for the betterment of my nursing career!"

"I want to lose, too. But I don't have anywhere we could donate the cookies like you did. How about freezing?"

"Let's don't torture ourselves! Only cookies better than warm from the oven are crisp from the freezer!"

"You're sooo right," Mia chuckled. "How about just coming over? We can make a salad."

"Yes!"

"Bring your ears. And your 'Sage of the Cafeteria' know-how. Something I want to talk to you about."

"You got it! See you tomorrow."

Mia glanced in the rear-view mirror. Peyton was

gazing out the window to the colored lights of the city.

The porch light was off at the house when she drove toward their little house, but the moon was peeking from behind clouds.

She hesitated, her eyes on the dark windows. She'd be alone there—alone with the night and her empty bed—undetermined future stretching out ahead.

My love, come down

Come whisper

with warm breath on my skin

How you are not gone

How I have only to wake from this long dream

to see you beside me

to reclaim our life

to settle the searing question in me

Where are you

Why did you go

What do I do now

Squirrels

Joyce arrived mid-afternoon with a sack of vegetables, salad dressings, cheeses, deli-turkey, croutons, sunflower seeds, and boiled eggs.

"Wow!" Mia laughed, "Are you sure we aren't feeing squirrels? You really did mean salad! BIG salad!"

"Figured we'd have fun making our own creations."

Mia nodded.

"So I want to hear what's on *your* mind, but *I'm* bursting at the seams! Want to hear something great?"

"Sure."

"I told you I'm applying to several nursing schools here in Seattle. I still have my job in Austin, but did you know my company also provides services in states all over the country, including Washington?"

Mia paused in making coffee to look at Joyce. "I didn't. But I know many communities have in-home care for seniors."

"I was wondering how I'll make the transition to Seattle, what my options for work here might be, and it suddenly occurred to me: I could transfer! Maybe I can keep my job and come sooner than later!"

"Oh! That'd help."

"I figured I'd throw it all up to God, the Universe, serendipity to work out details! Because I know help only comes to those who are actively trying to achieve something, I took a drastic step!" Joyce stopped chopping.

"What did you do?" Mia chuckled.

"I listed my house for sale."

"And..."

"It might be sold!"

"Just like that?"

"Yes, two days!"

"I thought we were in a down turn?"

"Guess it's priced just right!"

"I'll say! Geez!"

"The young couple is still in school, but getting

married and their parents are buying it as a wedding gift."

"Some gift!"

"Everything depends on their financing arrangements, but I'm hoping I'll be able to rent it back from them until I secure a job transfer."

"When will you hear about that?"

"I submitted a formal request a week ago, but I could hear any time."

"Will you live with Susan when you move here?"

Joyce laughed, "No! She needs her independence and I need space for all my things. I *will* pare down, eventually, but I'm not ready to part with my sewing and craft supplies and household items. I'll sort and recycle after the move."

"More plastic to eradicate?" Mia chuckled.

"Probably!" Joyce laughed. "Old habits creep back."

"I've moved more times in the past several years than I ever imagined. I recommend editing possessions often, again and again. Painful at first, but then so liberating. Take photos of special things, then donate or sell them to be utilized in new ways. Possessions hold energy and give energy. They also can keep us stuck..." Mia paused in chopping vegetables to look up with a passionate expression.

"You have grown! It's excellent advice. Thank you.

I will work on that."

Mia nodded with a look of satisfaction disturbed by a sudden yowl. Peyton threw a toy across his room and grinned when seeing her come in.

"Wow, baby boy, that was loud!" She changed him and carried him out. "Say hello to Auntie Joyce."

"Little man! Have a good nap?"

He smiled, but squirmed to be put down into the high chair.

Mia obliged, and brushed his cheek with her hand as Gerald often did.

Peyton pounded the tray for food.

She quickly brought over some cheese they'd cubed for the salad.

"Real food already?"

"Just yesterday, he refused to be fed. He did pretty well on his own with soup, but ohhh, the mess in the café."

Joyce laughed, "I remember David doing that. I had to hose down the tray, and him, several times a day! He was so interested in food I wondered if someday he'd be a chef or open a restaurant!"

"Yesterday, was hard. We drove up to Whidbey Island. A passing woman remarked that Peyton was cute, and asked if he is my 'grandson.'"

"Tactless."

"It shook me into realization. Time…"

"In what way?"

"Ahead: coming months and years alone."

"'Auntie' might be moving here soon," Joyce offered with a hint of optimism.

"Yes, that will be good," Mia sighed. "But, you'll be busy with getting settled, a new job, school if it happens, Susan, traveling back to Texas to see *your* son."

"True." Joyce finished piling a plate with salad fixings and dribbled on dressing.

Mia responded quietly, "I need to find a way to a new plan." She held up a glass of water, "Anyway, cheers to our last meal of the year."

"I almost forgot it's New Years Eve," Joyce said.

"Blue Moon—second full moon this month—happens only once every two or three years. The last one was the summer of 2007—just after I left Tim, and met Gerald."

Joyce nodded solemnly. "Besides being the second full moon in a month, isn't there seasonal significance of a blue moon?"

"Third full moon in a season of four full moons supposedly is a good time to set specific goals…" Mia sighed.

Joyce considered the next words, "Give yourself time to adjust."

"We had a future, plans, hopes and dreams," she whined. "I thought everything was as it would be. I thought all the light of goodness was shining down on us..." Mia blinked back tears.

Nodding with sympathy, Joyce said, "I remember feeling the same when we thought Neil had beat back cancer. Susan and David were busy with school events. We rejoiced in our health and goals. And then, Neil was suddenly sick again. We fought and fought, but cancer took him. I kept going for the kids."

"But *how* did you go on?"

"Simply, painfully, day by day, I continued."

Mia nodded, blinking glassy eyes.

They ate their huge salads, played with Peyton, put on a movie: *Sleepless in Seattle*. And cried throughout.

Sky changed to a new day, and another, and another followed in a blur. Mia kept close to home. Dish after dish appeared at the door. Gerald's co-workers, and a few neighbors who had previously been no more than familiar smiles and hand waves across yards and porches, now introduced themselves and inquired what Mia wanted in the way of lawn mowing or occasional babysitting or shopping.

Mia thanked them all, saying she'd call if there was need. But the only calls she made, other than to family, were many calls to remove Gerald's name from accounts. Finally, on January 19, 2010, the first anniversary of her marriage to Gerald, Mia reached the end of her "To Do" list. She marked the day going to Golden Gardens Park.

Rain was coming down. Tucked beneath the stroller was a box containing Gerald's ashes. Maybe she would disperse them, if the wind was right, if time allowed, if the shaking in her heart settled. Mia walked to the spot where they stood a year ago. She repeated the vows they'd written and the officiant had read because they were too overcome with emotion to speak. First the vows Gerald had written:

"I found you.

You are a gift.

You fell into my arms.

You rescued me from loneliness

and solitary pursuits.

Your touch filled me with new energy.

Let me show thanks to you every day of our lives.

You have my heart.

Be my love forever, my wife, Mia."

Tears slid down her cheeks just as they had last year. She wiped them away. And then Mia read the vows she'd written for Gerald.

"You found me in the darkness.

You lit the way.

I found peace in your arms.

You shared your heart and home and all you had.

You filled me with new life.

Let me give thanks to you for all of our lives.

Let me show you what love we can grow.

Say you will be my honey man,

today and every day.

Be my husband, my dear man, Gerald."

Then they had each said,

"I marry you. We grow together.

We are united in joy."

Mia smiled. "It's true. We can grow together. You're not really gone. I know you're with us. Maybe not every moment. But I think you know what happens with us. I think you can still influence our lives. I pray for your help."

Retrieving the box, holding it in her hands, she studied the Olympic mountains dressed in white, the white sky, the pale water reflecting the clouds. A crisp breeze blew.

But she shook her head. "I'm sorry. I can't part with you here," she whispered.

Mia pushed the stroller back to the car. But she did not drive home. As if pulled by invisible strings, she drove south. Stopping for gas, snacks, walking and playing breaks for Peyton to stretch his legs, she kept going until reaching the Columbia River. Turning east, she traveled the winding, windswept highway taken on that rainy night years ago when leaving the Portland gift shop in shambles.

After being relatively quiet for hours in the car, Peyton now fought restraint and created more fuss than Mia could appease with snacks or songs, so she stopped for the night one mile east of the small town of Stevenson, Washington. A winter special at Skamania Coves Resort allowed for a luxurious cottage with a view of the water. Outside, rain was coming down and spattered on the river.

After a dinner heated in the microwave, and a bath, Peyton went to sleep in the middle of the queen bed, while Mia sat up late in an easy chair. Her eyes were on the window and the dark water and sky outside. She slept, but fitfully with no dreams.

Peyton woke early. Somehow he allowed her to feed him yogurt and oatmeal, avoiding the mess he'd make in the room. She set him down and rinsed the dishes, turning just in time to see him pulling up on the ottoman and standing.

"Look at you, little man!" Mia swept him up and went outside, following a trail down to the water. "Isn't it pretty? Too cold and deep though," she said shuddering. "Shall we go on another adventure?"

"Bye-bye," he chattered and smiled.

Mia checked out of the resort, headed east again along the river. The hillsides stepped down to the water. Tunneling through fingers of rock, she honked the horn and Peyton laughed and clapped.

Further east, next to The Dalles Dam, a long bridge stretched above the river across to Oregon. She was unable to drive over it before, but this time Mia turned suddenly and crossed. "Look Peyton, we're doing it! This is the river where your daddy's ancestors lived and fished for thousands of years."

Down the city street heading west, she watched for Klindt's Booksellers, the oldest bookstore in the Pacific Northwest. A space right out front was vacated.

The glass door led inside. Her feet creaked across old wood floors. Her eyes scanned the perimeter shelves and there, under the fiction heading, was *Mending Stone*.

Her book in a bookstore!

Mia carried a book up to the checkout situated in the center of the store. Ms. Wande, the clerk met when Mia and Gerald had visited before, was nowhere in sight.

"Hello!" the clerk behind the counter said smiling. "Looks like you're in for good reading!"

She smiled, her cheeks coloring. "I'm Mia, the author of *Mending Stone*."

"Oh! My goodness! Welcome!" the clerk grinned.

"Thank you. I was surprised to see it on the shelf."

"We stock many books with local references."

"Ohhh."

"And also good fiction. I LOVE that book! I love the spiritual twists and turns, the mystery…I'm a fan of your writing!"

"Wow. You read it? That's sweet to hear. I had no

idea how it would be received."

"I couldn't put the book down! It was captivating! But I do have questions. I'm sure other readers will also. Have you considered writing a sequel?"

"Maybe…" Mia answered, paying for the book.

"Is this your son?"

"Yes, his name is Peyton. He's almost one."

"He looks like a good eater," the clerk chuckled.

Mia laughed, "He is."

"We're so happy you stopped by. Perhaps you'll be interested in an author event. At the end of summer, we'll gather together a number of Northwest authors with newly published books. Readers love to meet their authors!"

"I'd *love* to come," she gushed.

The clerk handed over the receipt for the book and a piece of paper. "Jot down your contact information. We'll be in touch in a few months."

"Thank you. And thank you for your comments about *Mending Stone*," Mia smiled, handing back the paper with her address, phone number, and email. Juggling the book bag, Peyton, and her purse, she turned to leave but stopped and asked, "I was wondering, is Ms. Wande here?"

"Ms. Wande?" the startled clerk echoed, shaking her head. "She's been gone for years."

Confusion showed on Mia's face. "Gone? We saw her here summer before last..."

"Oooo," the clerk shuddered, rubbing her arms. "If you did, it would be quite a memorable event."

"Ms. Wande was so kind and knowledgeable and had such a good connection with my husband, Gerald."

"They knew each other decades ago?"

"Decades? He did grow up here."

The clerk looked around as if someone had brushed behind them. "You *saw* Ms. Wande two years ago?"

"We *talked* to her."

"Oooo," the clerk shivered. "She passed in 2003. Is Gerald with you?"

Mia stammered, "He...passed..."

"I'm so sorry." The clerk recovered a tentative smile. "We'll hope to see you again. Keep writing."

Mia's brow furrowed.

On the way out the door, she stopped at the old gumball machine, slid a coin into the slot, and pulled the lever. Down rolled a yellow gumball she plopped in her mouth, and rolled the sweetness with her tongue.

As she drove from The Dalles, east along the Oregon side of the Columbia, Mia watched the sky and water whipped by wind. "Gerald, were you connected to spirits?

Am I? How did we see Ms. Wande? Was it imagined? Or magical?"

A few miles east, Celilo Village sat where Native Americans had lived and traded for thousands of years. Charlotte, Gerald's grandmother grew up there, but the falls were flooded when the dam was built. Not given tribal status, the residents at Celilo lost hope and their livelihood. And sometimes now, the wind blowing along the river sounded like weeping.

Ideas of dispersing Gerald's ashes in this ancestral place were abandoned when an osprey swooped down but continued flying upriver.

She drove on a few more miles and crossed over the mouth of the Deschutes River where it flowed into the Columbia. She could continue on the freeway to Biggs Junction and backtrack on the highway to the western shore of the Deschutes at Heritage Landing. She and Gerald had parked there and walked a quarter mile upriver to the spot where water swirled in a deep pool around rock, grasses swayed, and dragonflies fluttered beneath a blue blue summer sky—just like in Mia's recent dream. But now the sky was winter pale, and wind blew, and Peyton was heavy to carry any distance. Long gone were the summer days and Gerald's red tanned skin and the rivulets of water running from his pony tail down his warm back. The honey of his voice and the golden sun were far away and hazy as a dream.

She didn't backtrack on the highway from Biggs. And she didn't keep driving on to Rufus. Suddenly Mia turned around and drove back down the freeway along the gorge.

As she sped along, she did not give more than a passing glance to sites along the Columbia: not The Dalles, Hood River, Cascade Locks, Bonneville Dam, or Multnomah Falls plunging over the basalt cliffs. And her eyes did not linger on the river when she crossed it again and headed north. The twinkling skyline of Portland did not draw a glance to the rear view mirror.

Peyton fussed after each break from the seat and diaper change, but she played music and sang and talked and passed food and drinks back to him. Somehow they made it though the hours traveling back to Seattle.

But pulling up to the dark house, Mia suddenly arrived at a decision.

Next morning, she phoned Joyce. "Is your house deal going through?"

"The buyers want possession as soon as possible! *And* my job transfer is going through! I need to start ASAP!

YIKES! I need to move, now!"

"Would you consider house sitting for a while?"

"Where are you going?"

"I need dry ground and to spend time with family."

"I can be there in a few days possibly. David wants to keep a lot of Neil's things I can't part with, and he'll store the rest until I need it. Is that soon enough?"

"Joyce, you're a number one Godsend!"

"Goddess-send! A number one friend."

"Definitely," Mia replied with a laugh.

A few days later, Mia was stuffing things into a suitcase.

"What do I need?" she whined loudly, startling Peyton who played with the makeup bag she'd dropped and forgotten to pick up. She coaxed it from his hands and substituted a hair brush he quickly abandoned for hangers on the closet floor.

"Oh, my gosh! Honey! You're into everything! What will I do when you're really walking?" She hauled him out of her bedroom and deposited him in the high chair with a handful of cold cereal to munch.

Deena and Kelsey arrived and knocked.

She whipped open the door. "I'm not ready!"

"Can we help?"

"Yes! Locate the diaper bag; it's red. I thought it was by the front door, but I don't see it now."

"When did you use it last?"

"I don't know!" she exclaimed. But suddenly, Mia turned to look at Deena. "Oh. Duh. I brought it into his bedroom last night to load up! Geez. Thank you."

"We can start lining things up."

They shuttled bags to the door.

"These boxes need to be taped and put up in the attic," Mia said.

"Can I do it?" Kelsey danced with enthusiasm.

"Sure," she answered handing over the tape dispenser and scissors.

"I can fix Peyton a snack," Deena offered.

"Actually, I could use one, too. Feeling a little shaky." Mia pointed at the kitchen cupboard. "I took out apples and cheese to slice but got distracted."

"Understandable," Deena smiled. "Would warm milk calm your nerves?"

"Probably. Thanks. Good idea. I'm so lucky to have met you!"

Deena laughed, "In the right place at the right time when you came along looking for a house."

Shaking her head, Mia said, "I've never told you: I

wasn't looking for a house when we met. I was just driving around with Marisol and something made me pull over."

"A sign?" Deena suggested grinning.

"I only noticed it *after* I had a feeling I should stop."

"You're amazingly connected to spirit!"

"Maybe I just notice more than some," Mia shrugged.

"Keep at it. Something is leading you in helpful ways."

After drinking the warmed milk and eating some apple, cheese, and toast, Mia smiled, "I feel better. And I think we're about ready. Just need to change Peyton and go."

Kelsey and Deena drove them to the airport and said tearful good-byes. "If you're still there in the fall, we'd love to come visit. We'll miss you."

Mia nodded with wistful smile. "Kelsey, keep writing to Marisol. You're helping improve her English."

Kelsey grinned. "Our letters are helping me learn Spanish, too!"

Their bags were checked curbside. Mia lugged the baby through the terminal, and soon boarded the plane. Peyton squirmed incessantly on Mia's lap. "Oh, my gosh! You're so heavy," she muttered. "Like baby, like Mama.

We both could use more exercise!"

He puckered as if to cry and Mia quickly distracted him with a rice wafer she pretended to nibble.

He smiled and took it, but during takeoff, Peyton whimpered.

Covering him with a fleece blanket, she held him tight and he clung to her with the gooey wafer clutched in his hand.

"First time flying?" a man beside them asked.

Mia looked over. "I'm sorry if we disturb you."

The grey haired man faintly smiled while donning a pair of noise cancelling head phones, and closed his eyes.

"Technology's good," she breathed, and turned on a movie. Peyton was captivated by the bright images and was relatively quiet for a baby trapped on a lap.

Several hours later, after landing in Austin, Maggie and Angelo waved as they approached.

"Peyton! You've grown in only a few weeks!" Angelo said kissing them hello. "Darling, how was the trip?"

"Fine, Papa. Exhausting," Mia grimaced, pulling back the blanket about to drag on the floor.

"I have nothing I must do," Maggie claimed, "except baby duty if you want some rest."

"Thank you," Mia said. "I'm glad you both came.

We had to bring the car seat and I'm afraid I also over packed."

"Having what you need is good," Maggie smiled, her eyes on Peyton's rumpled shirt and dirty face.

"It's getting late and we should make our visit before supper. Tomorrow Mother has a doctor's appointment we couldn't change."

Mia's face flashed alarm. "Oh, no! Is she okay?"

"Arthritis doctors book months in advance."

Mia nodded, her eyes on bags coming around the carousel. She pointed, "There, with purple bandanas."

"Distinctive!" Angelo said grabbing the suitcases one by one.

They hurried out the terminal with Peyton fussing and started off in the car.

"Oh, no! I forgot to change his clothes!"

"I'll help," Maggie said.

When the car stopped at Angelina's, they worked to clean and dress him in a blue seersucker suit, brown and white leather saddle shoes.

"Adorable! Pastels are fabulous with his skin tone."

"I love this little suit. Gerald didn't like it at all, but I know Grandmother will! Nice enough for church; even came with a little hat, but his head is too big to wear it."

"Awww," Maggie grinned, kissing his cheek. "He does have thick, dark hair."

They went up to the house. Angelo opened Angelina's door with his key. They went inside to the study where Angelina was dozing in a wing back chair.

Mia's eyes filled with tears seeing her grandmother dressed in a silk blouse with cuffs and pointed collar, cardigan in magenta with a matching long skirt, stockings, and embroidered house slippers. Leaning close, she whispered softly, "Grandmother…"

Awakened, Angelina exclaimed, "Oh, my heavens! Look at your beautiful faces!" She kissed Mia on the cheek and held out her arms to Peyton.

But Mia set him on the floor. "He's too heavy and squirmy for your lap, Grandmother."

"A fine looking suit for a man about to turn one," Angelina quipped. She snapped a collapsed cane to straight, and struggled to her feet. "Look at these feet so crippled my shoes don't fit! Having a party and wearing house slippers," Angelina said exasperated.

"I remember wanting you to wear them all the time when I was little. I loved the embroidered flowers of satin threads! I wanted elegant slippers like that for my own!"

"You can have them!" Angelina cracked with disgusted tone, but smiled.

At the dining room table, a round pineapple upside down cake with caramelized brown sugar waited.

"Is there cream cheese between the layers?"

"Of course," Angelina smiled. "Your favorite, Mia."

Coffee and milk were poured, the birthday song was sung.

"I said there'd be cake!" Mia grinned at Peyton.

"Oh, dear. I forgot the whipped cream. Might as well have it. And the maraschino cherries. And brandy."

"Mother," Angelo objected.

But his mother waived a hand. "I'm close to one-hundred years old! I will have what I want! Who knows if I will live for another party."

"Mother, don't be morbid. Perhaps Mia will be re-turning in several months and we will celebrate all our birthdays together again."

"I pray it is so. But I am a realist. I've lived *this* long by facing facts."

Maggie nodded agreement with her mother-in-law, and Angelo brought over the requested items.

"Mia, Dear, I must say I am stricken with grief. Gerald was a fine husband. I'm sure he was an excellent father, as well. I pray he sees this fine celebration."

"Thank you, Grandmother. It means a lot to me to hear what you think of him."

"And you two made a fine looking young man."

All eyes turned to Peyton who reached out swiped a bite cake and ate it without getting any on his suit.

"He has tidy eating habits like his great grandfather, Federico, rest his soul. Except for eating with his hands," Angelina chuckled. "How long will you stay, Dear?"

"In Mexico? I'm not sure."

"Mexico?" Angelina's eyes flashed with surprise and irritation. "What's this you don't tell me? Keeping a secret from the old woman, Angelo?"

"No, Mother. Might have slipped my mind as we were discussing the party for today. Besides, it is for Mia to tell of her plans."

Her raised eyebrow hinted at disapproval, but Angelina rephrased, "How long will you be staying in Austin?"

"A few days, Grandmother. But they're all yours."

"Not running off to see your friend, Joyce? Friendships need care and feeding."

"I spent time with her recently. She plans to attend nursing school, has sold her home in Austin, transferred with her company to Seattle, and is house sitting for me."

"School at her age?" Angelina's brow raised.

"Joyce is no older than I was when studying for a masters in creative non-fiction," Maggie interjected.

"Does she plan to *use* her degree in some capacity, or does Joyce simply enjoy schooling?"

"Both, Grandmother."

"Women working into late years is not new. Women are the backbone of a family. A rib may have come from Adam to create Eve, but she was fashioned in beautiful strength with foresight of the Creator."

Mia laughed, "Grandmother, you are so right!"

"Always," Angelina quipped with a satisfied smile.

The next days, they visited a park Angelina enjoyed seeing Mia play in as a child, and they ate supper out at La Traviata Italian Bistro with Maggie staying behind to feed and watch Peyton.

"I'm finished!" Mia said pushing away a portion of her chicken Caesar salad.

"Good girl," Angelina praised. "A woman, especial-ly a widow, must mind her figure lest people think she's getting sloppy."

"What people? I'm not looking for a replacement husband!"

"Of course not, dear. You're still in mourning."

"Not *ever!*" But Mia unexpectedly broke into laughter, "Grandmother, you never change!"

"You will do well to consider your future and all opportunities. In every day waits fortune like a seed ready to sprout."

Mia sighed. "Thank you, Grandmother. I know you wish me well. I am a bit nervous about the future. One reason for spending time in Mexico: it's much cheaper to live there."

"Gerald was not well covered?"

"No, and though I received a judgment with the divorce from Tim, our money was lost somehow in the investment crash. He and Valerie and their son were barely getting by with the failure of the second store. Actually, my attorney said Valerie filed for divorce and is rumored to have replaced him with a wealthy and even older man."

"Oh, my. That is quite something. Some kinds of women," Angelina hinted with distaste. "Not enough to break up your marriage with her luring looks and ways!"

Mia shook her head. "There was much more to the end of our marriage than that, Grandmother. Without her influence, we might have weathered the storm. I doubt it though. But, without the loss of the marriage, I wouldn't have met my beloved Gerald, or written *Mending Stone*, and found Mama, or had Peyton and had this past year of such happiness."

"Something to be said for marital bliss," Angelo said finally joining the conversation. "*I* have never been happier. All the years with Victoria were filled with love, and she is in my heart forever. But these past several years with Maggie have also been truly remarkable."

"Oh, Papa," Mia whispered.

"All love is good and distinct and worth the price of pain," he advised with a softening look.

She swallowed hard and blinked back tears. "I doubt I will recover as fast as you did."

"A boy needs a father," Angelina declared.

"Yes, thank you. Your observations are noted," Mia replied, setting down her napkin. "I'll skip my usual *tiramisu*. I'm suddenly tired."

They drove to Angelina's, and then on to Angelo's.

Maggie met them at the door with Peyton walking with only two fingers for support.

"It won't be long before he takes off on his own."

"You're growing so fast, baby! Before we know it you'll be as tall as Daddy!" Mia said without pause.

"Dada! Dada!"

"Oh, no. Now I've done it!" She pulled a clutch of

photos from her purse and showed a picture of Gerald.

Peyton grinned. "Dada!"

Mia swept him into her arms. "We should turn in now. We have such an early flight."

"We wish you would stay. I don't understand why you have decided to go to Mexico, but we support your decisions."

"We couldn't upset your lives with an extended visit, Papa. And I couldn't stay in Seattle in winter. The rain and tears set me adrift on a sea of emptiness."

"You're such a poetic writer. I hope you will write more soon," Maggie said. "Perhaps the Mexican sun will fuel the words."

"I have no idea what the future holds for us."

"Give it time. The future will make itself known."

As she slipped into sleep, Mia's mind was filled with odd images of the mural Gerald had painted of the woman crying behind a wall of water. And then, another scene appeared: an orb of light pushing up through soil, blossoming, breaking free, and buzzing around like a bumblebee.

Gravity

Flights from Austin to Puerto Escondido were long hours with a baby on her lap, but Mia was armed this time with numerous strategies to occupy Peyton: fruit snacks, crackers, juice drinks, new little toys with moving parts, videos downloaded to her laptop, books to read, and a napping blanket. How she would manage to keep him on her lap was another thing! He periodically arched his back and pushed against her and twisted and pulled up on the seat in front of them. She could only resort to walking him up and down the aisles to stretch his legs and try to wear him out.

Thankfully, the woman seated next to them was friendly and laughed while introducing herself, "Evidently, my parents did not know how to spell Barbara! They named me *Barabara*, which I have learned is a sod or turf hut in northern Siberia or Alaska's Aleutian Islands."

"Funny," Mia chuckled. "Where do you live?"

"Puerto Escondido. Been there about five years. Love it. But, considering moving. Getting a bit restless."

"I thought I was the only one who does that!"

"What brings *you* to Puerto?"

Mia explained briefly about her mother's impending move inland to San Bartolome Quialana. "It's the village where she was raised. Her grandmother and many other relatives still reside in a family compound. It's quite basic, but filled with love. I visited a year ago for the first time. And last summer with my husband..." Mia started to say, but swallowed emotion before continuing. "Gerald passed away in December. It was sudden."

"Oh, no!" Barabara shook her head. "That's just the worst thing I've heard! I am stricken with sorrow for you and the little one!"

"Thank you, that's sweet," Mia smiled wistfully. "I grew up in San Antonio and Austin. Gerald was from the Northwest; we've been living in Seattle."

"Quite rainy there isn't it?"

"Lots of wet days. And nights. And days. But not as

bad as its reputation."

Barabara nodded, "Isn't that the way of most reputations?"

"Probably," Mia chuckled.

"What do you do? Besides raising an active child and keeping house?"

"I'm a writer. My first novel—*Mending Stone*—is published."

"How wonderful! I'll look it up! Are you working on another?"

"Only in my mind. It's gelling."

"I like that! Conjures pleasant and colorful images. What's it about?"

"That's difficult to answer. It might be non-fiction, something to do with possibility: making choices, growth, and rising."

"Rising? As in sun?"

"As in erupting from soil…"

"Ah! Interesting. What makes you a good writer?"

Mia thought a moment. "I love stories. I have an aching heart. And I'm observant."

"Necessary components! Can't wait to read you!"

"What do you do?"

"I'm a lover of beautiful things and finding homes

for them."

"So you're in sales?"

"I suppose so. An entrepreneur. I have a hand in many things around the world. Started a business in my twenties in Atlanta. Worked my way north, then west, far west, down under," Barabara flipped her palm as if it all required little effort.

"Sounds interesting. My first husband and I owned a jewelry and gift store in Portland, Oregon. I loved doing the displays, finding new products to carry. It was fun for a long time."

"What happened there? Get restless?"

"Actually, I think I did!"

"No crime in that."

"You're very open minded."

Barabara shrugged. "Does no one good playing the blame game. We're here to learn to do many things. Staying in one place or with one person does not usually enhance our capabilities."

"That's a refreshing way to look at change."

"Will you stay a while in San Bartolome Quialana? What will you do besides write and live with family?"

"Isn't that enough?"

"I wouldn't think so. But I haven't seen it or met

them either. Maybe I'll pay you a visit there."

"That'd be nice."

"Always looking for new opportunities."

"I'd love to discuss it more," Mia said shifting Peyton on her lap.

"Give me your contact information just for giggles."

They exchanged names and numbers and emails.

"Thanks, I feel better after talking to you."

The woman smiled, "I have that effect on some people. The rest detest me!" Barabara laughed. "Some just can't handle unabashed honesty."

"The opposite of how I was raised that's for sure," Mia laughed. "I take that back! Grandmother Angelina, is the same way. And I love her for it! I always know where things stand with her. No guesswork."

"It can be comforting," Barabara said matter-of-factly with a smile.

"Thank you for your patience with us. I'd better get him changed." Mia headed down the aisle with Peyton turned outward so he could see people. Passengers lining the aisle offered him high fives or smiles. "Peyton, Peyton, my little charmer!" she cooed in his ear.

Barabara was occupied with computer work when they returned to their seat. Mia watched a video with Peyton, this time he kept the headphones on his head without issue and eventually leaned back against her and fell asleep.

She breathed a sigh.

"Cute kid. Native American?"

"And Mexican."

"You could pass for different ethnicity: Spanish, Portuguese, maybe Italian."

"I did."

"It's the eyes. Lighter than expected."

Mia nodded. "That's the secret and lie I grew up with: I was told I'm Italian."

"Quite a ruse to pull off." Barabara stowed her computer. "When did you find out the truth?"

"Several years ago after Mother passed. I began writing the novel and questioning everything I'd heard and thought and felt."

"Love or malice?"

"The novel? It has both."

Barabara shook her head. "The lie?"

"Out of love, and fear of malice."

"Makings of a good story."

Mia smiled and prepared for descent.

The plane landed with a sudden bump, as if it could no longer resist the force of gravity.

"Ouch," Barabara complained. "Good luck to you, Mia Casinelli! Let's keep in touch." She gathered her things and squeezed into the aisle at the urging of a smiling male passenger.

Mia allowed most other passengers to exit, then lugged the baby and gear off the airplane.

Inside the small terminal, Javier and Rosalia were waiting.

Mia waved, and then caught a glimpse of a couple involved in a heavy kiss. She could not turn her eyes away from Barabara and a handsome, blond, and deeply tanned man in his mid-twenties.

Barabara turned, noticing Mia and said, "Meet my boyfriend, Carlo."

"Pleasant to see you," she managed, and colored.

Laughing, Barabara responded, "I see I've rubbed off on you! Can't say anything but the truth!"

She laughed, "Hope to see you again."

"Mutual!" Barabara turned back to her companion.

Mia went over to her family.

"Make friends?" Rosalia inquired.

"Maybe. Thankfully made a long trip much more interesting."

"Hope daughter rest! Many things need do now!"

"I'm ready for work! It'll be good to dig into a big project!"

The next day was spent packing. It was slow going with Rosalia unusually concerned over every item.

"Mama, pack *everything*! What you don't need personally can be used for classes and donated to the community center."

"But expense great for take all this!"

"Tally the value of the donated items to use at the school and the cost of getting them there and include all that in the costs for the establishment."

"Daughter have good influence in business."

"How are you planning to transport everything?"

"Javier have friends. Some with trucks. Travel day after tomorrow."

"We're packing up the kitchen; what will we do for cooking in the meantime?"

"Surprise!"

"Oh, really? Okay. We can pack all but the bedding and essential clothing. If we have time, I'd love to spend some time at the beach tomorrow."

"Make time. Baby need air, and feet in water!"

Mia and Peyton slept in the little casita outside the main house with the sound of waves rushing and receding like music on the beach below. And words came to her with ease.

> Sorrow and rejoicing exist together
> Influx and efflux
> necessary process of growth
> Change a given
> Be thankful

When the packing was finished the next afternoon, they went down to the beach. Peyton splashed and played at the water's edge until exhausted and falling face down into the warm sand. When Mia retrieved him and headed toward the trail up the hillside, Peyton let out a yowl and struggled to break free from her grasp.

"Oh, my goodness, baby! You are getting so strong! Maybe I *will* be happy when you walk safely everywhere on your own and don't need to be carried!"

That evening they went out to eat at La Olita on Playa Zicatella. Its atmosphere was comfortable and festive, and though it was quite crowded, the waiter immediately led them to a very large table put together along one wall. As they were being seated and Mia was strapping Peyton into a child seat, others filled the remaining chairs. When she looked up, Mia's face showed surprise at the many familiar faces: friends of Rosalia and Javier, including Dr. Grimaldi.

"Lanzo, I'm happy to see you."

He leaned down and kissed her cheek. "I am deeply saddened to hear of your loss. Your husband was a good man. It is a tragedy. I only wish I had a chance to be of some assistance. Was it his heart?"

She nodded, suddenly unable to speak.

"Perhaps a cardiologist's arrogance, always supposing he might have made a difference." Lanzo added, "I'm sorry for your loss."

"Thank you. Your kindness means more than you know. And yes, if only we had known something was amiss…" Mia's eyes studied his face and the tender concern in his look. "You saved Mama. Perhaps…"

"May I sit beside you?"

"Oh, of course," she managed to say, clearing the chair beside her of Peyton's diaper bag. "No *Lady* with you today?"

"No," he chuckled. "In rather dramatic fashion, she showed she was a bit less of one than previously thought."

"That's funny," Mia laughed, but then caught herself and apologized. "Was it difficult for you?"

"No, in times like that, parting is rather a relief. Your mother tells me you are off with them to San Bartolome Quialana tomorrow."

"Yes. I arrived here on short notice. Suddenly I could not face winter weeks and months of Seattle rain alone in a small house with an active baby."

"How long will you stay?"

"I really have no idea. Thought I'd play it by ear."

"You play very well," he grinned suggestively.

Her cheeks colored. "Thank you, Lanzo. You do have a way about you."

He nodded, smiling.

Fish tacos, shakes, fruit, and yummy crepes arrived to the table and they ate family style from the offerings. There was much laughter and many well-wishes for Rosalia and Javier.

As the dinner wound down, and Lanzo prepared to leave, he said, "If ever I could be of service again, I should very much like to have time with you, Mia."

"Thank you, Lanzo. You know you have meant something to me. Probably you have not seen the last of us. Let's leave it at that."

"Delightful. I shall await the day," he said bowing slightly, and departed after giving instructions to Rosalia regarding her medical care.

Before going back to the house above the beach, they stopped at Carmen's Cafecito for dessert.

Mia had chocolate-chocolate cake.

"I'll worry about the calories and my figure and tomorrow, or not at all," she said while drifting to sleep with no dreams or visits or other words in her mind.

Humans

The drive over the mountain road inland was slow and
winding through lush forests of green. The road was in as
poor repair as it had been when they traveled it before. But
thankfully, they could drive slow, avoiding potholes and
animals in the road. Still, Mia let out a long held breath
when they were finally down to the Oaxaca Valley.

"I like this open landscape, Mama. I feel like I can
breathe again. I don't think I like the tropical vegetation of
mountains and coast. It's overwhelming. So dense and dark
and drippy."

Rosalia nodded. "Pretty grass and hills here make
heart happy. Look like home!"

"Is everyone excited about us coming?"

"Wishes come true! Family happy, change house. Javier build something. Maybe for daughter, too."

"OH! I didn't think about that! We were visiting last time; probably everyone scrimped on space they normally use. Does it take long to make changes?"

"Cousins have young men for help. Many hands make quick work."

"I hate for them to bother making changes for me if my stay is short."

Rosalia shrugged. "No matter. Find place for daughter and baby now, maybe add more later."

Nodding with her face showing emotion, she said, "My life now is so drastically different from the years in Portland, and growing up in Austin. I hardly think I'm the same person. It feels as if I'm emerging from a confining illness to find I was sustained by love and support of people I did not know were there waiting for me."

"Like this with Javier. Heal, help, and love."

"Do you ever think of my father and wonder what actually happened to him?"

Rosalia's eyes showed a far away glimmer. "Sometime think hear Mano cry. Sometime think see in dream." Rosalia shuddered, "But different. Face with scars like a ghost."

"Oh my Gosh! I saw a man like that in Oaxaca City! A crumpled man was blocking the sidewalk where Joyce and I were walking. When I tried to pass, he grabbed my leg and wept, and he said…"

Rosalia shuddered again, and interrupted, "No good from this! Someone, something take Mano away. Javier husband now. Time of Mano go."

"That's smart, Mama. You're the wisest human I know. I'm lucky to have found you."

Excitement built as their vehicles proceeded through Tlacolula de Matamoros and on into the village of San Bartolome Quialana. Heads turned. People appeared in windows and doorways and waved and smiled.

Mia laughed with glee. "Look!" she said pointing down the street at Marisol and Benito. As the caravan slowly passed, kids thumped the vehicles with their hands and ran alongside. A small crowd followed. The trucks and vans, four in all, came to a stop outside the family compound. Well-wishers greeted them. "Like we're some kind of celebrities!"

"Businesswoman! Authoress! Contractor! Bring excitement to village!"

Family rushed out, hugged each of them, and the carrying began: personal bags and food first, then other things were unloaded and stacked inside the gate.

Later, a celebration ensued. People filed in with food and drink to share. It was crowded and noisy. After the varied food offerings were finished and dishes cleared away, musicians began playing. There was much singing and even some dancing. These festivities were nearly as great as the joint wedding had been in summer.

Nothing public was said about Gerald, but one by one people approached Mia and relayed how sorry they were for her loss and many tears fell.

Mia and Peyton were put up again in her great-grandmother's abode. *Abuelita* Inez slept in the main house with her daughter, Rosalia's aunt, *Tia* Patrice. Mia object-ed, saying she and the baby could certainly share the space with *Abuelita*, but everyone insisted it was best for Mia and Peyton to have quiet and privacy.

As she lay with her son on the pallet on the floor. With the sound of music and laughter of the party still ring-ing in the air, Mia quietly prayed to *La Virgen de Guada-lupe* and the Blessed Mother.

"Are you separate, or two personalities of one?"

She prayed thanks for the safe passage over the

mountains, appreciation for the gracious welcoming and generous feast filling more than physical need.

And Mia prayed for a visit from Gerald. Did he safely transition to wherever spirit goes when it leaves this world? Did he know where they were?

"How I miss you," she cried softly. "Unbelievable to be here again—not even a year after our wedding—and you are gone." Tears soaked her sleeve where her head rested. "It's all so strange."

Though she said she'd return to the party, Mia could not leave Peyton sleeping alone. She rested on the cushion, and her eyes studied the stucco walls of the old hut, the rough hewn wood door, the rustic table and chair. Slowly, her eyes became heavy, and she slept with dreams.

He walked ahead on the trail beside the river.
She hurried, but his strides were long. A
breeze rustled leaves tumbling alongside, and
lifted her hair. Her eyes looked at the water
swirling around a huge stone with a long crack
down the center. Her eyes lingered there. An
insect—blue like sky—fluttered nearby. Her ears
took in the rushing river. Her back was warm.
She smiled and turned, but he was gone.

Morning brought sounds of the village to Mia's ears. She opened her eyes. Peyton was still sleeping, arms thrust out, his mouth moving as if chewing. Mia smiled, her finger lightly stroking the soft palm of his little hand. "It's all ahead for you little one. How does a woman raise a good man, a kind and giving but strong man like your daddy?"

Weeks passed, and no answer came.

Mornings when Mia got up and washed her face in a basin of water, she asked, "Is this our life? Dirt floors, no running water in our room, only a toilet and shower to share with many others here, and isolated from the world?"

But when Peyton awoke, the wondering would wait.

Often, she followed the trail to *Ahuehuete*.

Mia sat under the tree in the shade of spreading branches and she spoke quietly.

"I've missed you, *Ahuehuete*. I was away—away in my heart and mind. I'm thankful for all you've been to me. I don't mean not to pay attention, but we're so busy living. I was so busy with Peyton and Gerald making our family and our home in Seattle. I don't forget you, but other things are more present in my mind. And my heart is occupied. Sometimes I can't feel you, can't tap in where you are in that space of knowing. Am I wrong and somehow neglectful? Is that why my Gerald went away?" Mia sighed with great passion, "Have *you* also gone from me?"

She stared up through the tree's branches. Did the leaves shudder with heavy emotion? Or was the fluttering shaking off her words?

"Blessed Mother, you know my heart. You know I do not mean to turn from you. I am only busy helping my dear ones. I don't think it is selfish, is it?"

Her eyes looked in the distance to the dark mountain, Picacho. Black like 'black stone,' the meaning of qui-alana in the native *Zapotec* language. A steadying influence. Her roots were here with ancestors at the base of the mountain in this community. What were the cultural expectations for her? The family was Catholic. She was raised Catholic. And Gerald was, too. Would she raise Peyton in that religion? Or any other? Would she let *him* choose his beliefs?

"Is this my place to be? What am I supposed to do?"

The word *supposed* caught on her lips. She shook her head.

"I don't need *permission*. I don't need to do what may be 'expected' by anyone, even my family. I *can* make my *own* way, my own truth. I don't fit *here* more than I fit in Texas or Oregon or Seattle. Family can be of blood or heart. And goals can be my own, if only my wants will be known."

Winter of want

heart of spring

can expressions of hope

be grown

from fragile extensions

hair-like stretchlings

reaching for wet

wild tangles of growth

twining through rock

Several months passed. Rosalia sewed and developed new designs.

Mia worked with the family, played with Peyton as he grew and developed, and she spent time with Benito and Marisol and taught them what she could.

Javier built another bathroom in the compound. He added a room for sleeping. He built an outdoor storage area of cupboards and shelves next to the corner where large quantities of food were prepared. Efficiency was enhanced by these modifications. He added several closets, a window to allow light through a dark wall. Family praised his efforts and the speed with which he worked.

Talk about the proposed community center spread slowly. It was a radical idea. *Zapotec* people generally did not instruct their offspring in ways of doing. Offspring were expected to quietly watch and learn. Tradition was passed on by habit. New ideas were foreign. And though Rosalia was one of their own, this man she brought was not. Javier, was from the northern state of Michoacan. However, he was endearing himself to all with his hard work and polite talk and offers of help. Requests began to multiply. Javier did not charge money for his work, so long as food or other goods were traded fairly. He helped in any and every way other than farming which was not known to him. He was a hunter, a gatherer, a self-made entrepreneur with many skills. And it was not long before he was accepted fully.

Rosalia's business "partner" who discovered her excellent sewn items while on a scouting trip to Puerto Escondido several years before, had been selling them at the *Angelita* stores in the United States. David came to meet with her to discuss new business ideas and the Puerto Escondido shop she left under management of a woman named Florentina. David proposed an expansion in that shop and developing additional markets such as Oaxaca City which was only twenty-two miles away from San Bartolome Quialana.

"For this, much work. Hands and eyes tire. Need assistants sew."

"That's a very good idea," he answered, nodding his greying head.

"Bigger space for sewing and cutting. Equipment: sewing machines, scissors, tables, pins, paper for patterns."

"Are you talking about a piece work factory?"

Rosalia shook her head, "Community center for training with internships. Less pay needed. Teach sew, how work at business, and other skills."

"That's an interesting idea."

"Perhaps government give money for this. San Bartolome Quialana high in numbers leaving. Farming difficult for women with duties to home and community. Many need work to support family after men go."

"I see," David replied, a hand stroking the stubbly hairs on his chin. "How many people could you train?"

"This village more than 2,000 people. Maybe find twenty or fifty to learn and work."

"That many?"

She nodded. "Some work for wage. Some supervise. Some purchase fabric, supplies. Some sell at markets. All learn how do everything."

"A good strategy for continuity: educate each person

in all facets of the operation. You'd need classrooms, work rooms, offices, store rooms."

Rosalia nodded.

"At least a few thousand square feet. Two stories to minimize the footprint. What is the cost of land here?"

"Man die. Have no children, but wife like village and sad young people leave for city. If have school and work here, maybe stay. Woman give building for work and learn."

"Hmmm. A civic minded benefactor. How expensive is construction?"

"Javier good contractor. Many men have little to do, work for reasonable rate."

"You'd need an architect for changes to the existing structure."

"And money for building materials." Rosalia shrugged with a smile. "Maybe application easy for native born."

"Let's hope."

"Have great hope! And determination."

David studied her. "I believe you mean to do this, with or without me."

"Partner? Match money government pay?"

"What payoff for my investment?"

"Make budget together. Five year business plan. Most profit go for payback, some for changes, and growth."

"No offence, but how do I know you have five years in you to work, or live?"

She responded quietly, "Same age? Maybe David have five years, or more?"

"Good point," he chuckled.

"Family invite for dinner tonight. Ask questions. Decide."

David smiled.

He came to the family compound in the evening and was greeted at the gate.

"Welcome," several excited teenagers said, and escorted him into the courtyard to a large table with colorful flowers dressing the center.

"This is lovely. Thank you for having me."

Rosalia and Javier introduced David. A frothy drink of passionfruit was shared.

"Later, toast business with *mezcal* (liquor made from agave)?"

"If we reach agreement."

Rosalia indicated Mia down the table. "My daughter, Maria Isabel Angelina. And our grandson, Peyton."

David nodded, smiled Mia's direction. "Maria…"

"Mia," she offered. "Mama speaks highly of you, David. I appreciate your care and distribution of her work. Several years ago, I happened onto your attractive store in the mall in Austin."

"Thank you. My honor and pleasure to work with your mother. She is a gifted craftswoman and a talented businesswoman as well."

Rosalia smiled, and volunteered, "Daughter have many years experience in gift store in Portland, Oregon."

"Very good. Will you be involved in this business venture, Mia?"

"Only in a supportive capacity. I currently live in Seattle."

"Nice city. If all goes well, perhaps we'll finally expand into markets in the Northwest."

"You *are* thinking big."

"Possibilities are endless. But there are many considerations. And I am concerned about the welfare of all."

Rosalia took Peyton from Mia's arms. "Go now for *Abuelita* Inez."

A few minutes later, Mia returned with her great-grandmother, Inez. David was introduced, and Inez smiled and nodded.

"*Abuelita* work hard many years. Many women in

village work as many," Rosalia claimed.

"Your longevity is certainly well represented by this beautiful lady."

"*Gracias*," Inez responded when his comments were translated.

They soon began eating red *mole* on pork, black *mole* on chicken, squash blossom soup, and squash with *queso* (cheese). Tamales stuffed with raisins, coconut milk, and cinnamon were dessert.

Conversation was light and friendly with much emphasis on questions from the young people about the United States. David was quite informative and his colorful descriptions and obvious love for his country piqued greater interest.

"I had planned to return to Texas tomorrow, however, I've been in touch with an acquaintance from the States who'll be nearby and we'd like to do some sight seeing."

Mia smiled, "There are many interesting places to visit. What do you want to see?"

"Somewhere called the 'water boils' sounds intriguing."

"We've been there and love it!" Mia replied.

"Would you like to come along?"

"Oh! I…" Mia glanced at Rosalia.

"Go! Many mothers, many arms care for baby!"

Mia looked over at David, and back to her mother. "I would actually like to go very much."

"Good for daughter!"

"It would be several hours of travel. And I'd also like to see other local markets and ruins," David said.

"Oh, yes," she replied suddenly hesitant. "You should see Mitla."

"Good research for these business proposals. We could book a hotel for a night. Of course I'd secure separate lodging for you."

Mia nodded. "That would be necessary."

"You could act as my tour guide," he suggested, his clear blue eyes without a hint of deceit or threat.

"Could someone else come with us to make a better appearance?"

"Of course, if you wish," David answered politely.

After some debate though, an escort was deemed unnecessary since both Mia and David were American citizens and no cultural norms took precedent over the situation, and Mia was agreeable to the arrangement.

David lavished great praise on the family for the meal and the floral arrangements in abundance. "I've been blessed with beauty, delicious food, great kindness and welcome," he said with a wide, white smile. "May we step aside Rosalia and Javier, and have a business discussion? Mia, would you act as witness?"

They took up seats on benches along the back corner of the compound where it was quiet and shady beside a potted bush of *salvia adenophora* (Oaxacan Red Sage) in full bloom with clusters of tubular red flowers.

"Lovely color and form with many blooms. I hope they are good symbols for our new ventures! I've considered your general proposal and would like to go ahead with drafting a business plan, contacting an architect for renovations, and developing a bid for costs. Do we agree to a tentative partnership?"

Handshakes and toasts with golden caramel vanilla *mezcal* followed.

Excitement ringing in her voice, Mia congratulated them, "Mama, Javier, David, this is tremendous! I'm so impressed and excited for your new endeavor!"

Rosalia responded, "Perhaps daughter join?"

"I might consider later, but right now I have no feeling about proceeding toward the future."

"Take time. Political matter maybe long."

"What politics?"

"Oaxaca traditional. Communities treat women different. Changing many men go United States. Many leave San Bartolome Quialana, send money back for families. But still women struggle."

"Exactly why the training center is needed! Practical education for women and girls is important. But I hope other educational opportunities will develop with extended cooperation with other communities—maybe in the U.S. as well as in Mexico."

Rosalia shrugged, "See what happen."

And smiling, they rejoined the family in the courtyard for singing, music and dancing late into the evening.

Jay

Mia woke before sunrise. She slipped out, and found her way through the darkness to *Ahuehuete*.

"Are you here?"

A breeze blew across her bare arms.

She sat beside the tree.

"I don't know why I want so badly to go on this excursion. It's probably selfish and silly. And inappropriate. But I want to go. I shouldn't burden Mama with Peyton overnight, but I *need* this. I need time away. I've been going, going, and going and not breathing or thinking or feeling and now I need something...I need time away from loving eyes of family and friends. I need space between us.

Space to recover something I've lost…"

Be well.

Tears streamed her face.

"Oh, Gerald. My honey man. I miss you so! It's a comfort being here, but these women are so deeply entrenched in old traditions. I'm not like them. I don't know what is to be my future. I need to find a path to something more."

Bird chatter in a nearby tree grew louder.

Mia's eyes searched for the source of the sounds moving closer and closer. A blue jay dropped to a bush, and then the ground. He crept toward her. "Hello," she whispered, holding out a hand. "I have nothing but myself to offer." The dark eyes studied her, then the tail flipped, and the jay flew up into the lightening sky.

A dog barked in the distance.

Mia smiled. She finished a prayer for safe travel and care for Peyton, then returned to the compound, and quietly packed while he slept on. Soon she was ready to go and he woke.

Rosalia was up fixing breakfast.

"Mama, I hope Peyton is okay for you." Her face

showed tension and worry as she handed him over.

"Nana Lia's dream: hold baby day and night."

Laughing, Mia said, "I doubt you could hold him that long! Peyton is so strong, and except when he is nearly asleep, he really does not like being restrained. He wants to be down and doing!"

Rosalia only smiled and began giving him food. "No worry. Be well."

Mia stared a moment, then leaned down and kissed their cheeks, and rushed out before tears fell.

She met up with David at the gate, and got into the car with driver.

"We'll find my friend, have a bite to eat, go to *Hierve el Agua*, then go back to see the ruins and marketplace at Mitla later," he suggested.

"Okay. Where is your friend from?"

"California? Colorado? Traveled around some with various positions."

"How do you know each other?"

"We met years ago. An outdoor event of some kind," David shrugged. "We get together every year or so, somewhere we happen to be. We enjoy exploring new places. Hard to find other adults who travel without difficult agendas and requirements."

"I suppose it is. Making lasting friends is also difficult for adults with active careers and lives."

"Agreed."

"Hard to find a match of interests and dedication."

He nodded. "What's your story? I sense there's a lot I don't know."

"Ohhh," she sighed, and glanced out the window at the landscape. "I was raised in San Antonio and Austin."

"That would be the Texas accent I detect."

Mia nodded. "I guess it's still with me. I left college to marry. Tim and I bought the jewelry and gift store in Portland."

"What happened there?"

She sighed again. "It was a good place for business. We did well and were expanding to a new store in the area. But a combination of factors..." Mia turned to meet his eyes. "Fifteen years of too much work and not enough fun, lost babies, a new young employee on the scene complicated the success of the marriage, and not long after, the business as well."

"Hmmm," he growled.

"I hadn't noticed how narrow my life had become, how isolated. My marriage was done, I just hadn't realized it. I went back to Texas to spend time with parents during

Mother's illness. And moved there after..."

"Mother? Wait. Isn't Rosalia your mother?"

"Yes, but I didn't know it then. I was raised Italian. I didn't learn the truth of my heritage and parentage until after Mother died and I started putting pieces of the puzzle together."

David gave her an apprising look. "When was this?"

"Two years ago."

"And since then?"

She glanced up to his blue eyes. "It's been complicated." Her eyes turned to gaze again out the window at the dusty landscape of agave and sparse vegetation. Soon tops of buildings came into view. "Oh, look," she pointed and smiled. "There's Mitla!"

"Striking."

The driver pulled to the side of the road at Hotel Don Cenobio located in the village of San Pablo Villa de Mitla, 44 km from Oaxaca de Juarez (Oaxaca City).

"We'll stay here the night, if this is acceptable?"

Mia nodded. "Let's go see."

The rooms were done up in gold and cobalt blues and flowers were in abundance.

"Nice! Later, I'll be sleeping in elegant beauty."

"Glad you like it," David replied smiling. "Let's

make room in the trunk for potential purchases."

They retrieved their things from the waiting car, and met up a few minutes later at the café.

As they walked in, David scanned the room, and started toward a table at the back. "Hello!" he said patting a shoulder covered in sun-bleached hair.

The head turned, showing a brilliant white smile on tanned face. "You made it! And with company!"

David laughed. "This is Mia. I'm business partners with her mother, Rosalia."

The stranger nodded, flashing another disarming smile and pale blue eyes with golden flecks. "I'm Jay! Pleasure to meet you."

Mia recovered enough to respond, "And you." She commented to David as they took seats, "For some reason, when you were referring to your 'friend,' I thought it was a woman."

They laughed and Jay replied amicably, "Definitely not a woman!"

Her face colored. "Of course, I see you are definitely masculine, and so…muscular."

Jay smiled at her.

The waitress came for their orders, and they were soon having *tortas* (sandwiches).

"This is really good," Mia said after a few bites of hers filled with avocado and tomatoes.

"Are you vegetarian?"

"No," she said. "It just sounded good. "And truthfully, I'm wanting to scale down a few pounds. I still have baby fat to lose," she said but grimaced over the unexpected candor.

"Oh, you have a little one?" Jay asked.

"Yes, Peyton. He's fourteen months."

"Fun age."

"About the same as my grandson," David offered. "You have kids don't you, Jay?"

"Boy and a girl." He pulled out his wallet and showed two photos. "Twelve and ten. They live with their mother in Colorado."

"Oh," Mia nodded, watching Jay closely.

"I have them six weeks every summer and shorter visits throughout the year. Miss the daylights out of 'em!"

"I can imagine. I'm close to a girl and boy in San Bartolome Quialana. They stayed with me in Seattle a few months last year. They're seven and four now. I'm looking forward to my son growing and doing more with them."

"It happens quick! Does he take after his father in ways? Do you see what type boy he is?"

Her light brown eyes flashed. "What *type*?"

"Outgoing, shy, athletic, studious…"

"Oh. I don't know yet," she answered.

The two men caught up on recent events, and when all had finished eating, Jay inquired, "Shall we go, Mia?"

"Sure," she responded, smiling over at them.

David led the way out to the car. Soon they were en route to *Hierve el Agua* in the rental car—David in the front seat with the driver, Jay and Mia in the back.

"I gather from the lunch conversation you're with family in Oaxaca?"

"Yes," Mia answered. "My mother and her husband have moved to her hometown from Puerto Escondido."

"How long will you stay?"

"I'm not sure. I…I'm in a state of transition." Her eyes studied Jay's face. "And grief."

"How's it going?"

"What?"

"The grieving process. What have you learned?"

She thought for a moment. "I've grieved before, but this time is different."

"How?"

"I'm keeping active, reaching out more, trying to accept what is my life now."

"Not so much, 'Why me? Why did this have to happen?' type questions?"

She nodded. "Hard to let go of that though."

"I lost a good friend last year in a tragic motorcycle accident in Nevada; he was killed instantly. I was planning to see him the next week. I did a *lot* of questioning—going over and over the details as if trying to discover some small nougat to make sense of it all. Maybe trying to bargain: if only I could figure out where it went wrong, we could go back and recover lost plans."

She nodded, her mouth a thin line. "We make plans, but life intervenes."

"And death," Jay added.

Mia rubbed her arms, shaking off a chill from the familiar statement she'd made to Angelo. "Last time I grieved for babies lost in miscarriage, a husband lost to divorce, and the only mother I'd known lost to cancer. How'd you lose your children's mother?"

"Not that dramatically. Catherine and I knew early on we'd make good partners, but we also knew we wouldn't stay together, so we didn't marry. It's a complicated way to make a family, but not sad. We both got what we wanted. And the kids are developing well and happy."

She was nodding as the car that'd been winding up a

narrow mountain road came to a stop in a parking lot.

"Photos I've seen of this place are amazing!"

"I've been here several times. It is magical," Mia said getting out of the car and pulling on a hat with floppy brim.

"Can you see from under that thing?" Jay teased.

She smiled.

They made their way over to the edge of the cliff and looked to the valley below.

Jay said, "Wow! Where's my hang glider? Maybe I could use Mia's hat."

"Always pressing the limits," David chuckled.

"Do you prefer wind tangled hair and blazing sun on your face?" Mia smiled back.

"*Touche*! I probably should wear a hat also," Jay grinned. "Keep my youthful good looks."

They went to the "falls" and marveled over the beautiful formations. The trail was handled easily. They cooled off with feet in the pale pools of water after.

"Let's get something to drink," David said, and went to fetch cups of *pina loca* (pineapple, *mezcal*, and chili) from a vendor. "Whoa!" he said taking a drink.

Mia sipped, and smiled. "Sooo good!"

"Yep! Makes me want to dance!" Jay commented

with great exuberance, and they all laughed.

They spent some time soaking in the beauty of the place.

Later, back in San Pablo Villa de Mitla, they had a lively meal in the restaurant at Don Cenobio. The décor, and one mural in particular of flowers and grassy hills and trees, Mia said represented what she thought Italy would be.

"Much of it is like that," David replied.

"You travel a lot, don't you?"

"Always looking for great products and opportunities for new markets."

"What do you do, Jay?" Mia asked.

"I'm a brew master."

"That's interesting."

"I came to Oaxaca to learn more about *mezcal* and other types of beverages."

"How does one learn to do that kind of work?"

"I went to school for Fermentation Science. Took a lot of post graduate courses in craft beers, owned a tavern in Portland a few years."

"Oh, you did? I lived and worked a long time in Portland."

"Do you like Voodoo Donuts?"

"Of course!" Mia laughed.

"I heard they have plans to open one in Denver. Can't wait to take the kids there!"

"Voodoo Donuts?" David asked. "Do they cast a spell on eaters so you can't get enough?"

They laughed, and Jay answered, "You'd think so! They're *that* crazy good!"

"Strangest flavors imaginable! But so delicious!" Mia chimed. "I'd love one right now! But, I need to break the sugar cycle of ups and downs. I'm in the process of change, trying to find more balance in all ways."

"Diet is one way to reestablish body connections. Grief underscores discovery: we can't control everything, can't know where lives might go. But we can find balance."

Mia sighed, looking into Jay's blue eyes. "It's hard to surrender, learning to let go of how we thought things would be."

Jay nodded.

"What you asked before—what I've learned about grief. I think I know now. Last time, I thought I recovered because of Gerald. I thought he saved me, brought me out of suffering. But now, I know it wasn't him."

"How do you know?"

"Because," she said, barely audible voice catching in her throat, "this time, I grieve *him*. He died unexpectedly a few months ago."

"I'm so sorry," David said.

"Yes! Terrible!"

She swallowed, blinked her eyes. "I realize now, it was me all along: *I* healed myself. I ran and cried and cooked and allowed creativity to flow through me. I *will* run again, at least walk," she smiled. "And I'll cook and create. I feel Gerald's influence, and sometimes I sense he *is* with me, but it's *my* strength I'm relying on. I feel myself returning to someone I recognize, and going forward, someone I want to be. Someone starting to come into focus..."

"Who is it?"

"I'm not exactly sure yet. Last year, I was so busy getting to know my mama, helping Marisol and Benito, marrying Gerald and making a life together and having a baby. My first novel was published. Now a new chapter is hatching inside me."

"I have no patience for writing words," David commented. "I rush through what I must put down. I far prefer studying numbers and financial strategies." He paused. "That reminds me, I have something to tend to." David stood and shook their hands. "Enjoy dessert or drinks on me! Shall we meet for breakfast and be off for the ruins and markets?"

"Yes," Mia answered. "Thank you. Good night."

Jay grinned, "See you in the morrow."

"Oh! *You're* coming with us tomorrow?" she asked.

"Better with you two than on a stuffy tour."

"Okay then!" David waved and walked away.

Mia said, "When I came to Mexico the first time, we had a guide with knowledge of history and tradition, but I found it difficult to pay attention. I was distracted by the 'feel' of the places. Her voice and constant instruction interfered with something else seeming to speak to me."

Jay smiled at Mia. "Maybe something will speak to us tomorrow."

Her eyes studied his look. "Do you want coffee or a drink or dessert now?"

"I could use a walk."

"Fresh air would be welcome," she said standing and leading the way out of the restaurant.

They walked up a narrow road lined with businesses along one-story concrete strip mall type block buildings.

"The colors are pretty, even in this light."

"Architectural detail lacking but paint scores!"

She laughed. "You and David seem good friends."

"We're friendly acquaintances. I like his easy going way. Not too uptight for a businessman. Seems on the level.

Trustworthy."

"He does," she nodded. "He's done well with Mama and her craft."

"Creativity runs in families."

"Maybe it does." Mia paused and looked up at him.

"Want to go back?"

"Yes," she answered, turning around at the end of the line of buildings. "It's good talking to you."

"Where's your room?"

She told him the number and they walked there.

"We're practically neighbors," he said stopping at her door. His hand touched her hair, his fingers spreading and pulling through a length of dark strands. "Pretty."

"Thank you. I'm letting it grow to donate for wigs for people with health challenges."

"That's cool." His blue eyes met her light browns. He smiled down at her.

They leaned, their lips touched.

She pulled away, opened her door, went in and closed it behind him. Somehow, they moved across the room.

Mia might have pulled away. Might have stopped kissing him. But she didn't. Their bodies pressed together.

His voice was asking, "Yes?"

Her voice might have been silenced by memories of other lovemaking, but it whispered, "Yes."

She might have been too self conscious to risk him seeing the pounds she wanted to lose. But she wasn't. Her eyes were open.

So were his.

He held her to him.

Their clothes came off.

Their bodies sought the bed.

The air conditioner was not yet on, and sweat dripped as if washing away all that'd been before.

Their bodies found a way together.

Laughter rang at possibly awkward moments. But they were easy together—*he* was easy on the eyes, easy to be with, and *she* was, too. Though they moved with vigor, the responses were unhurried.

After the sighs of release, and tears, they stretched out with pillows under their heads, and talked a while.

"Okay?"

"More than," she smiled, turning her face to him.

He kissed her forehead.

"You're sweet."

He kissed her lips. "You're sweeter."

"I could taste you all night—like dessert that's better

with each and every bite."

"Ho, ho!"

She laughed, "I'm glad you're not a woman."

"I'm glad *you* are!"

"Do you think David had this in mind when inviting me to join you for the outing?" Mia asked suddenly.

"We could ask him."

"Oh, no!" she sputtered. "I don't know him at all really. I don't want any kind of discussion about *this* to come up with him, or my mama!"

"Not to worry." Jay kissed her cheek. "It's just ours."

"Thank you," she smiled, and yawned.

"Do you mind if I go now?"

"No. If you stay longer, we won't sleep and I'll be too tired tomorrow."

"Sensible. I like that," he smiled, dressed, leaned down and kissed her hair.

"Good-night," she said softly.

As Mia drifted toward sleep, her mind let go of the images of Jay, of their bodies entwined, of thoughts of him. It shifted to Gerald. She sighed with the memory of his strong and quiet ways so filled with intention and connection, and words were in her mind.

My love falls

like petals in the wind

soft and sweet

But then questions slipped into her mind with other words.

The scent of you

sense of you

Why didn't I know

Why didn't you say

Why did you go that way

slipping away in the night

while I was sleeping

still lost in dreams of what might have been

She cried then. Not from shame or regret over what she'd just done or that somehow the memory and love of Gerald was violated. But because tears fall, springing from the source, dripping down like *Hierve el Agua* washing over a precipice.

After breakfast in the morning, the trio wandered through the marketplace near Mitla. David stopped at every clothing stall to examine the stitching and sizing and embroidery of articles. "None are as precise or finely crafted as Rosalia's. I'm pleased to find our *Angelita* line truly is the best available."

"Are you convinced the center will be a good undertaking?"

David nodded, "Getting there."

"How about something to drink?" Jay asked, eyes scanning for a vendor selling the cups of froth in the hands of passing tourists.

"That would be welcome refreshment."

They found a stall, and purchased fruity drinks.

"Sweet," Mia said taking a sip.

Jay smiled at her and raised his cup.

"Hmmm," David remarked with keen awareness. "What are we toasting?"

"Fun and new friendships."

Mia tapped her cup to theirs. "I loved seeing *Hierve el Agua*. I've been a little homesick for the Northwest and all its bodies of water."

"Ever visited Central Oregon or Washington? The eastern side of the Cascade Range is dry like this."

"I'm embarrassed to say I've taken little time to explore. I've only been as far as up the Columbia River

Gorge as Rufus. I did love seeing the mountains from Portland," Mia agreed. "And the Olympics I see from Seattle are striking."

"Do you like geology?" Jay asked.

"I don't know much about it, but I do appreciate form and composition."

"Landforms are part of geology. A lot to explore in Oregon. I'm captivated by the many different formations and the bodies of water."

"I've seen the Willamette River flowing through Portland and meeting the Columbia. I've been to the mouth of the Deschutes."

"That's a good river. Lot's of little tributaries with crooked gorges carved through stone."

"Plenty of good places to see everywhere." David interjected. "I prefer California: warmer weather and water, lots going on, more business opportunities."

"You're a good entrepreneur, David," she said. "What about brewing, Jay? Are there many business opportunities?"

"Oh, yeah!" he remarked. "That's why I came down here looking for a new idea, something unique for crafting a signature brew."

"That sounds challenging," she commented.

"I love the creative process. I'm on the edge of discovering a great new combination. I can feel it!"

"What will you call it?"

"Possibility! After a song by Lykke Li written for Stephanie Miller's *New Moon*."

"I love movies," Mia said. "And music, but I haven't heard that song, or seen the movie. The Twilight Series sounded too dark."

Jay shook his head. "A love story with all the drama of decisions: cling to the past, or move forward with a possibility of new love. But with vampires and werewolves thrown in," Jay laughed.

"Too far out for me, too," David said finishing his drink. "I'm off to look at more vendors."

"We'll check out the ruins."

"Fine. Let's meet up in two hours. Then we should be heading back to San Bartolome Quialana."

"Okay," Mia nodded, but her eyes were on Jay's smile. "I do like the name for your signature brew."

Jay nodded. "Thank you! I've been considering the concept for a while. But it seems the time is right now. I'll see what else I happen upon down here."

"I'm learning about possibility." She paused, looking at him. "I wrote a poem about that once. Do you understand poetry? Or are you more of a black and white, no symbolism type thinker?"

"I like some. That's why I like song lyrics; they're poetic forms."

"I've always thought so. That's part of why I like movies—for the music. It's expansive. It allows us to stretch and grow with the notes and arrangements. We can travel to different places in our emotions. And I think creativity is sparked."

He watched her with keen interest.

"I didn't suspect, growing up, how even subtle limitations keep us from daring to stretch and grow and dream. I tried to keep within bounds—acceptable in every way. And in the process, I became unable to even *feel* my own wants and needs, let alone act on them. I lost hope. Then there was Gerald. I thought he changed me. But I realize now, it was me changing, opening to what was all around."

"Possibility exists everywhere in everything."

Mia nodded, "That's what my friend Joyce says."

"Let's hear it."

"What?"

"The poem you wrote, if you can remember it."

She studied him, as if to detect some mockery, but his only expression was interest. "Okay, here goes:

My Momma told me to be a good girl

a nice girl, a do-as-I-should girl

Momma told me, 'Be quiet. Be a lady:

thoughtful, kind and sweet.'

Momma told me what I should not be

what I could not be.

Momma told me everything

I thought

except what I could be

and the possibility

I could be more

than a GO-ALONG girl."

Her eyes watched his face for a response.

"Packs a bit of a punch."

"Does it?"

"Yep. What was the relationship with the mother who raised you?"

"Um, I'd say confusing. I thought at the time, difficult. Now I realize it was quite loving. But the secrets she kept wore away at her. I never felt I knew or understood her and thought she felt the same." Mia sighed, "I was wrong about that. Mother risked everything for me and loved me in every way she could."

"Good to discover that kind of love, even if late," he said, smile on his tanned face looking bright in the sun.

"Yes," Mia nodded. "Though she's passed, now I tell her what I feel."

"That's good. Death isn't an ending, just a change."

"That's what I think, too," she said quietly.

They walked through the ruins, their eyes studying the intricate and ancient designs of carved and fitted stones on walls and ceilings.

"I love the patinas: colors so warm and weathered and soothing," Mia said. "I've always loved stones; they're solid, each unique but with similar base characteristics."

"Now you sound as if you do know something of geology."

She laughed, "Not really. I'm more of a generalist. But I do pay attention to texture and color. Do you ever feel as if stones speak to you?"

"Of course! One reason why I love the Oregon desert lands. Especially Smith Rocks where morning and evening colors are displayed on the massive walls," Jay stated enthusiastically. "Stones have special powers for us."

"What powers?"

"Clarity. Strength."

"I have two stones I found by the Columbia: rounded, smooth, and dark with streaks of light running through. The shapes are like a mother and baby. Their discovery was part of my journey with grief, writing *Mending Stone,* finding my heritage in Mexico. Maybe *they* helped usher me from grief."

Jay quipped, "Powerful rocks! Cool you recognize the influence. You're very tuned in."

"Is that what it is?"

"One way of describing earth element connections."

They were walking beside round pillars in a narrow, open air room. She stopped to touch the massive stones. "I'd love to build something with stone. Maybe only a wall or walkway in a garden. I'd love to collect stones everywhere I go and make a winding pathway." Mia paused and smiled over at him. "Natural elements speak to me. Sometimes I wonder why I think I like living in cities."

"Maybe you're changing. Maybe becoming a nature girl." Jay's blue eyes were noticing her cheeks, color of her lips and dark hair pulled back in a plain black band. "Natural things appeal to me, too," he said warmly.

Lizard

Mia pushed open the gate and ran into the courtyard. She scooped up Peyton who was playing as Rosalia sewed.

"Oh, my little darling! I missed you so!" She set him down, and embraced her mother. "How was he?"

"Angel no cry. No fuss. Only sleep peaceful and long."

She sighed, tears springing into her eyes. "That's good. Though I'm a little sad. Didn't he miss me?"

Rosalia shrugged. "This one, warrior. Have great courage."

Mia nodded, examining her child's dark eyes, thick hair falling on his neck, his skin now colored deep reddish-tan by the Mexican sun.

The next weeks were filled with contacts, compiling information David needed, continuing the process of gaining public acceptance for the school. A general atmosphere of vitality and excitement was growing. Architectural plans were drawn and approved. Permits were acquired. Work began on the building. Unemployed workers who had been idle now donated their time and skills. Javier was a good carpenter and contractor; he gave clear instructions to the labor force. The construction project was nearing completion by the end of July. Many women helped organize the materials for the school.

Mia helped plan the interiors with cheerful, colorful, and dynamic visual elements such as murals, mobiles, stained glass type paper projects for windows. She tapped her inner artist utilizing numerous techniques: sewing, collage, painting, and decoupage. Old furniture was donated and refinished and revitalized.

A contest was held to choose a name for the facility.

"I have best name," Marisol claimed.

"What is it?"

"No tell! I win contest, you see!"

Mia laughed, squeezing Marisol's shoulder with a hug. "I hope you do!"

The proposed names were presented and reviewed at an open community meeting. School of San Bartolome Quialana. Learn, Grow, Prosper. Light of Hope School. Learning and Living Community Center. After much animated discussion, votes were taken. Number one choice was a combination of several proposals: Light of Quialana Community Learning Center—LQCLC.

Marisol danced on happy feet after the meeting. "Maybe I no win, but I say 'light' and they use! I say, 'Light of Hope School,' and they like!"

"Yes, light is a perfect beginning for the name. Light represents hope!"

"Hope like star bright?"

"Yes. And *you* are bright, Marisol! You light my life," Mia said with great warmth in her voice. "Both of you do!" she said hugging Benito and Marisol.

"When Mama Rosalia start classes? I want learn so much!"

"We still have many logistics to work out. We need to appoint supervisors and train teachers."

"Aunt Elodia teach!"

"She does?"

Marisol nodded. "Before marry, she teach cooking to women."

"Ask make presentation!" Rosalia said.

Marisol beamed. "Teachers make money?"

"Not exactly. There will be little or no tuition for students, but everyone providing a service will receive credits for themselves or others they designate," Mia explained. "They can use credits to purchase goods produced or services provided by the center."

"Okay. I tell Aunt Elodia!" Marisol responded, and hurried off with her cousins and Benito.

Peyton was fussing and rubbing his eyes and getting into boxes and emptying contents on the floor.

Mia exclaimed, "Oh, boy! Mama, I need to go put him down for a nap. Can you handle this without me?"

Nodding, Rosalia waved them away with a smile. "Go! Carmen and Nicolasa help."

"Good," Mia sighed. She held Peyton's little hand and they slowly walked down the street toward the family compound. When he faltered, she carried him, shifting his weight from side to side. It was warm with the sun high, but clouds were gathering. Already the air smelled of rain. Drops would fall on the dusty streets. It was rainy season in Oaxaca, but the temperature here at over 4,000 feet was milder than at sea level in Puerto Escondido several hours south.

She put Peyton down in their room at the back of the compound—the room her great-grandmother had vacated more than six months ago.

"Oh, Pey-Pey," Mia whispered, stroking his forehead with her finger. "Do you like it here? Do you like all the people and activity, the food and sounds? The dust and the sun?"

But he was sleeping, and he did not yet have more than a dozen words to speak, though he sometimes said them in either English or Spanish or the native tongue of *Abuelita* Inez and the family who were of *Zapotec* origin.

Mia closed her eyes and slept, too. When Peyton woke from his nap, she changed him, and wandered out to the kitchen of the main house. "Hi, Mama."

Her mother's eyes rested on her face. "Daughter have question?"

"What question?"

Rosalia shrugged. "Something bother."

"The school is ready to launch. Your volunteers are in place. My job here is finished. I'm restless. I need something more. I thought I could start writing, but the words won't come."

"Time go north?"

She nodded, eyes glistening. "Almost."

Rosalia reached out and wrapped arms around Mia and Peyton. "Okay. Go see."

"See what?"

"See what heart say when there again."

"Mama, you are wise and kind. I love you."

"Always mama's girl!" Rosalia smiled. "Be happy."

Mia smiled, "It's what I want for all of us."

Light of Quialana Community Learning Center opened days later with several dozen students, young and old, in sewing and pattern making classes. A week later, Mia was preparing to depart with Peyton. Family and friends gave them a sendoff dinner.

"When Mia came, she look like this…" her young cousin, Otilio, said making a face like a deer with wide eyes frozen in headlights.

Everyone laughed.

"Feet wear clean white shoes and little socks. But now," he pointed at her feet, "sandals dirty with dust!"

They laughed again.

"And first here, Mia wear big hats over face, and cream for sun protection every inch of body. But now, see how brown. Like us! Peyton, too."

Everyone nodded.

"Now they go to U.S., and we miss them. We pray be well. We pray return here to forever home."

Glasses of assorted beverages were raised but their faces held the same look of love.

Mia addressed the gathering, "My heart has grown large with your caring. I leave a piece of it with you like a seed of hope. Love can grow unimaginable-before-dreaming kinds of wonderful things. Be curious. Help each other adapt and change. With love, we have everything!"

The crowd clapped, and Mia went around to speak to each person before retiring for the night with Peyton.

Early in the morning, Mia made a last visit to *Ahuehuete*. She knelt at the base of the old tree.

"Mother, you weather the years. You offer wise counsel and solace."

A lizard ran from beneath a bush.

Mia pulled a spoon from her pocket and tried to dig, but the ground was packed and hard after rains. She opened the box she carried. Inside, a zip-locked plastic bag with printed trademark name caused her to pause. She drew a breath. Her fingers slid the zipper. She stood up and looked around, then began to pour. A sudden breeze lifted her hair and swirled the ashes, dispersing the tiny grains.

Mia smiled, tears in her eyes. "Just like you, Ger.

Always with your own way of doing things. Be happy. Be free."

She shook the bag one last time. "*Ahuehuete*, please watch over my beloved Gerald and the family here when we are away."

Leaves shook on the tree, though there was no breeze.

Turning, running the trail back to the family compound, she whispered, "Blessed Mother, guide our way forward."

Mia had the window seat on the flight to San Francisco. Her eyes fell to the deserts and mountains below and then the water of the Pacific Ocean when she could see it over Peyton's head resting on her shoulder or chest.

"Hello, my country! Hello, California," she said with gaiety.

"Away long?" asked the passenger in the next seat.

"A lifetime it seems."

"Where will you go?"

"When?"

"In San Francisco?"

"Oh, I don't know. I don't live there. I visited only a few days two years ago. I went to the zoo, and drove to

Quarryhill Botanical Garden."

"Lovely."

"Do you live or work in San Francisco?"

The woman with grey hair pulled back in a bun and deep brown eyes nodded. "I'm a practicing psychologist."

"Where were you in Mexico?"

"San Miguel de Allende. There's a sizeable ex-pat community. I own a small home there and travel down to stay a month out of every six. It keeps me sane," the woman said, eyes twinkling. "Eventually I'll retire to spend half my time in Thailand, half in Mexico."

"It would be an interesting life!"

"I always follow my interests. What do you do?"

"I'm a mother, writer. My first novel came out months ago, but I've been singularly focused on family."

"Congratulations on your child and the birth of your book! What is your next project?"

"I think it's a non-fiction piece."

"Oh? What subject?"

Mia thought a moment, "Rising gifts of grace."

The woman nodded. "Gifts of grace—like being able to focus on one thing at a time? That's a priceless gift. Call the book, *One.* I'll watch for it."

"That's kind of you."

"I have a feeling all will be well," the woman said with great conviction, smiled at Mia, then began collecting her things as the plane touched down.

Peyton began crying and Mia tried futilely to soothe him.

"Good luck," the woman uttered.

Struggling to reach her own things, Mia glanced over and said, "You, too!" But the psychologist was already up the aisle.

"What's the matter, little one?" Mia asked Peyton. "Thankfully, we're done flying. Are you hungry?" She offered a puree of spinach and fruit he gulped down while other passengers crowded the aisle.

"Goodness, I'm sorry. Are you better now? We can go in just a minute." She wiped his face, lifted him to set him in the woman's vacated seat and he vomited all over the front of her. "Oh, baby," she sighed.

Inside the terminal, Mia went to the ladies room. She set Peyton down and provided distraction by placing the diaper bag in reach. He pawed through it while she wiped at her shirt. The spinach and fruit he had eaten was not easily removed. "Why didn't I bring another top?" she whined, close to tears and dabbing at the stains. "I *knew* I shouldn't pack all my things in checked baggage."

A woman with short blond hair had emerged from a stall, was washing her hands in the next basin and noticed Mia's struggle. "Traveling with a little one is tough, huh?"

Mia nodded, extending her palms in a gesture of helplessness. "I was planning to grab a quick meal before I get our luggage, but I couldn't possibly eat with this on me! It smells disgusting and looks unappetizing!"

The woman dried her hands, glanced in the mirror at her own carefully arranged outfit. "Here," the woman said removing her top two layers. "Take these. The blouse is light, but you can put the scarf over it."

"Oh, no, I couldn't!"

"I'll wear this." The woman pulled a sweater matching her pressed slacks from her large purse and put it on.

Mia still hesitated.

"Go ahead. I'm not a weird stranger. I'm Randi, just a sister with a shirt and a scarf."

Mia laughed and accepted the items.

"See, now that we're friends, you can take the clothes off my back," Randi chuckled.

"It's so generous of you," Mia said, removing her vomit covered top. She put on Randi's blouse and draped the patterned turquoise and orange scarf over it. "This is so pretty. I feel honored to wear it. Thank you. I'll send them back, I promise!"

Randi shrugged. "Really lovely on you with your coloring. Wear with joy. Keep them, or I can give you my address if you feel compelled to send them back," she smiled. "Why don't I come along to help manage your things while you get a bite to eat?"

"I couldn't ask you to do that."

"You're not asking, I'm offering."

"Thank you. It would be such a help."

A short distance through the terminal, they found a restaurant. "What do you like?" Randi asked glancing at the posted menu outside.

"I could eat anything really."

Randi led the way to a table inside while lugging Mia's diaper bag and her own large purse.

They sat down, and ordered drinks the waitress brought immediately.

"Where are you coming from?" Mia asked.

"I've been in the Orient."

"Oh, that's interesting. I just met a woman on the plane who hopes to retire partly in Thailand." Mia's bagel and cream cheese arrived and she chopped pieces for Peyton. "We've been to Mexico. We have family in Oaxaca."

"I've been there. I travel extensively. I was a travel

writer for years. It was always interesting."

"I'm a new writer with a published novel, *Mending Stone*. It came out, but I'm finding it difficult to get enthused about marketing."

"I'm branching out in new directions now. I have a publication you might find helpful." Randi gave Mia a card with her address and links to her blog.

"Thank you. This is all very helpful."

"That's what I do. I like to think I'm a cheerleader for other women making connections, finding inspiration and ways of moving forward. It's a LOT of work, but I love what I do."

"I love being a mother, writing, and doing other creative things. I'm still looking for some other..." she breathed. "Something."

"Decide what you want; focus on that one thing at least a few minutes every day."

Mia nodded, "Right! *One*. My word for the day. Have you always been so outgoing and sure of yourself?"

"Oh, no! I've worked tremendously hard on that. Many, if not most of us, have suffered through things. Right? We've struggled to feel good enough, strong enough, smart enough to even *live* our own lives and make our own choices, let alone thrive in them!" Randi said with a gleam in her eyes.

"My confidence has been shaken so many times! Just when I think I have something conquered, another thing comes up."

Randi smiled. "Yes. I'm constantly striving to improve and innovate, to be better at things I do. But, life does intervene. Events and incidents, especially with family give us a good shaking. We need to constantly adjust and re-evaluate. It's not easy to stay on top. And sometimes, the things we want most, must take a back seat to things we need to do for others. It's our job to learn how to navigate through this life. We have only this one right now."

"Yes. This life *is* a creative process. Possibility is everywhere."

"Endless."

"Yes," Mia sighed. "We're here to find more."

"That's RIGHT!" Randi agreed loudly.

They laughed, finished their drinks, put money out for the tab.

"Thank you so much, Randi. Your efforts are generous and kind. And talking with you has renewed my spirit."

"Good luck with writing and marketing. Let me know if I can help in any other way. Consider including your novel in one of my upcoming publications. Read about them on my website."

"I will. Thank you, again."

"A pleasure to meet you, Mia. Have a safe trip, wherever you happen to go. Bye-bye, Peyton," Randi said waving before leaving the restaurant and disappearing around a corner.

Mia gathered up her son and struggled with their gear. She started toward the baggage claim and noticed someone with a cart. "Where did you get that?"

"Available free for international," the man replied pointing in the direction of a stack of carts.

"Oh, bless you!" she grinned.

Mia rented a car. "Why not take a scenic adventurous route home with my best boy?" she said glancing in the rear-view mirror for Peyton's reflection in a small mirror hung over the back seat so he could see himself and her reflection, but he was watching out the window.

Driving fast, she turned on the radio. A station of "oldies" was playing popular songs.

"Oh, Gerald," she sighed listening. "These songs remind me of your cabin, the first weeks I knew you. Three years ago everything in my life was turned upside down and now it is changed again."

Ingestion

Vineyards crept up the hillsides of California wine country with orderly rows of controlled growth in the right balance of sun and water for ripening grapes. Mia's mind flew back to the Maryhill Winery vineyard on the windswept Washington hills of the Columbia River.

Who tended those grapes?

Who nurtured those fruits to sweetness?

Who provided tender care allowing the grapes to develop?

Did the grapes know when receiving the best care?

Did she?

Mia sighed. Peyton was sleeping and she couldn't

stop driving or risk a grumpy boy, but somewhere between Santa Rosa and Healdsburg he did wake kicking and fussing and struggling with the restraints of his car seat, and it was impossible for her to drive much further.

There were probably dozens of charming Victorian houses converted to bed and breakfasts for tourists and travelers to stop for the night, but a toddler in close quarters was not predictable. Mia opted for an attractive motel, Dry Creek Inn, on the north side of town.

After Peyton had stretched his legs running back and forth on a patch of grass outside their room, they headed to a local grocery. She purchased food and drinks for supper and breakfast. After carting in the bags and the boy, Mia checked the television service in the room. Quite a few movies were playing, including a couple of children's shows.

"Darling boy, I hope you'll be tantalized by colorful images and music. Mama wants to watch television!"

She warmed food in the microwave, and propped him in a vinyl barrel chair at a little round table. They ate while watching Disney. By eight o'clock, Peyton was fast asleep on a floor bed of a cushy comforter folded over several times.

A movie played with the volume on low, but Mia

could not keep her eyes open. She woke repeatedly, checked on him, slipped back into slumber. A strange dream like a poem played in her mind.

Gnarled tree swallowed up

Ingestion by molten lava

Liquid fire morphing into stone

Cooling wind

Golden sun rising over red rocks

Blue falling from the sky

cutting with a curving tail of water

across desert land

Next morning, armed with brochures from the motel lobby and Google search information, she decided to take a wine country route north and south again along Alexander Valley Road.

"So pretty, Pey-Pey! Don't you wish we could pick some grapes?" She grinned at him in the mirror. "Probably not as good to eat as for sweet adult beverages. Someday you can try them. Don't worry, it won't be long. Before we know it, you'll be running off to make your own life. I'll try not to be heart broken and missing you too much."

Vineyards, winery tasting rooms with attractive decks and patios, in rustic or Victorian style architecture mixed in an elegant patchwork of romantic settings with flowers blooming in abundance.

Deciduous and evergreen trees covered the mountains separating northern Sonoma County and the Alexander Valley from Napa Valley. She followed the road over the top of the Mayacamas Mountains and down to the lush green tilled fields of the Napa Valley. A small town was situated at the north end. "This is perfect," she grinned driving into Calistoga and spotting a play area. "Finally, Peyton! Something for you!"

They ran on the green grass. He giggled as she pushed him in a bucket swing. Stairs to the slides and the ground cover were challenging to navigate. He stumbled and fell a few times, but Peyton only laughed and got back up, unconcerned by the brown bark clinging to his clothes. After more than an hour of playing, they were both sweaty and tired.

Loaded back in the car, he sucked down two fruit and vegetable squeeze snacks, and drank a cup of almond milk. Mia ate a handful of nuts and drank a water, then resumed driving. The little main street of town was lined with shops and businesses. There were restaurants and spas and soaking facilities with mud baths utilizing nearby mineral springs for relaxation and healing.

"How about a mud bath?" Mia giggled.

Watching her in the mirror, he laughed.

"Clap for yes! Clap, clap!"

He chuckled again.

At the eastern edge of town, the road split. She followed the way north. It was steep with hairpin curves and extremely narrow lanes.

"Not fun!" she complained after having to swerve to avoid a boulder in the road with tailgating traffic pushing faster and faster.

Reaching the top of the hill, she breathed a sigh of relief with wider lanes and fewer turns. But vehicles pulling out of hidden driveways behind hedges caused traffic to suddenly slow, making unexpected hazards.

"Why'd I want to do this? Oh, yeah, I wanted more adventure. Ok, we came, we saw."

She drew a breath when Clear Lake came into view. Motor boats were speeding around on the water. "Oh, how I would like to swim, but not with all that noise! When we get home, maybe I'll sign us up for lessons at a pool."

Farms and fields and oak groves were passed, and finally the freeway was reached. "Look at all the fancy cars and giant trucks! What money and commerce we have in America," Mia said, but the sound of traffic and air conditioning had lulled him into quiet, so she drove fast. "Probably not the wisest choice driving hours and hours with a toddler. Thank you for being so easy now, baby!"

At Corning, California, she pulled off for gas and continued to a local business. Getting out of the car, they were hit with heat magnified by the asphalt parking lot of The Olive Pit. They went inside and devoured cooling ice cream, then browsed the aisles of consumables and household items.

"Look, Peyton. Isn't this funny? All the olives are turned so the pimento stuffing is looking out like eyes staring at us! Peep! Peep, peep!"

He laughed and laughed each time she said it.

"Wouldn't Papa like this?" Mia bought a jar to keep for Angelo's next visit.

Back in the car, she looked up mileage to Seattle. "Ten hours on the freeway? That's too far to go today; we'd better drive more though." Looking at the map, she picked a spot and drove two hours to Mt. Shasta.

A 'laid back' and funky vibe predominated in the quaint town. She found a comfortable and quirky hotel: the Swiss Holiday Lodge with an outdoor pool, hot tub, and a small view of Mt. Shasta. Little snow remained except on top of the massive volcanic peak standing 4322m high. "I've seen pictures! I wanted to see this impressive mountain! Check off another site on our list!"

There was nothing watchable on the television in their room, so Mia loaded Peyton up, and they went off to town. They walked up and down an old street lined with funky shops radiating a "free-spirited" vibe selling crystals, minerals, jewelry, and other "spiritual" items.

Eventually she found some wooden blocks and a colorful pop-up book with turtles and whales to buy for Peyton. In another shop, she discovered a pile of whistles and couldn't resist blowing one with the head of a bullfrog. A croaking sound blasted out.

Peyton laughed out loud.

"That's hilarious!" another shopper laughed.

Mia turned to stare into friendly green/blue eyes of a red-haired woman. And then she noticed the necklace the woman was wearing. "That is really beautiful."

"Thank you," the woman beamed. "Don't you just love the feel of stones?"

"Yes, I do!"

"Oregon Sunstone and pearls, with the center drop of citrine; I love the gold shining through. It spoke to me!

And I love how it makes me feel!"

"I know what you mean. My friend gave me a necklace of rainbow moonstone. Whenever I wear it, I feel kind of magical."

"Rainbow moonstone has awesome properties; it balances and clears your aura, and helps with the timing of things—perfect when making decisions. It also improves focus when you're struggling mentally."

"Seems focus is a popular word!" Mia chuckled. "Several people have mentioned it."

"Maybe trying to tell you something."

Mia rubbed her arms and shivered. She looked around. Peyton was handling felt puppets in a display.

"Sorry," she said to the clerk watching.

"Little ones can't resist playing. Those are samples. We have others in boxes up on the shelf."

"Smart," Mia smiled with relief showing on her face. "Probably sell more with kids falling in love with them! This is pretty," she said admiring a puppet with stars in its hair and a shimmering brocade costume.

"Might help tap into your goddess energy," the lively shopper said smiling.

Mia's brow furrowed.

"Moonstone is a very feminine stone, and is in

touch with goddess energy that's fabulous for helping with creative projects and getting rid of writer's block."

"How'd you know I'm a writer?"

"I'm intuitive. I give readings. And I'm a gemstone empath; I give workshops, make jewelry…"

"That's interesting. What's the name of your site? I'll look it up."

Handing Mia a colorful business card, the woman said, "Gemstonealchemy.com, formerly Bold Bodacious Jewelry. I'm AnnaMariah."

"Oh, my gosh! *YOU* made my moonstone necklace! Joyce bought it from you for *me!*"

AnnaMariah laughed. "I love it when this happens!"

"Do you live in Mt. Shasta?"

"Nope. Just down for the day to recharge at the mountain."

Mia gave the necklace AnnaMariah was wearing another look. "You have a way with stones."

"I love how different combinations enhance the beauty of each stone, and add to their properties. There's a perfect combination for every person."

Peyton began to push and pull against Mia, and she said, "Guess we better go."

"Have a great night. If you get a chance before leaving town, stop by The Crystal Room. It's an amazing store with eight rooms of gemstones! *And*, it has awesome crystal bowls—even one in moonstone!"

Mia was making her purchases and nodded. "It was surprising to meet you. Thanks for the information."

"Remember to wear your moonstones soon," replied AnnaMariah smiling.

"I *will* wear them! Maybe they will help bring me to my next…" Mia paused, "decisions."

AnnaMariah laughed heartily, as if sharing a tantalizing secret.

While walking to the car with Peyton, Mia checked the sidewalk behind several times, as if expecting someone to appear, but there was no one.

She drove over to the Wayside Grill advertised on a flyer posted on a bulletin board in one of the visited stores. Soon she was carrying away a to-go order of award winning lobster bisque and freshly baked bread wafting the scent of warm butter and yeast.

"Peyton, Peyton, Mama needs to diet when we get home! But tonight I want comfort food," she sighed.

They returned to the motel. After eating, they played with toys, danced again and again to "chicken dance" music on her phone. Finally, she plopped Peyton into a warm bath.

He splashed and grinned and drank water from a cup while she looked on from a perch on the toilet lid.

"So this is my life," Mia sighed. "I'm sure you'll be quite the conversationalist soon enough, but ohhh, how I would enjoy some adult conversation."

When Peyton was dried and diapered and dressed in pajamas, she tucked him into a cozy floor bed with the stuffed turtle and whale book at his side.

She reclined with pillows on the lumpy bed and sipped a glass of sweet and mellow red wine, not the Prosecco she drank most often. She phoned Joyce. "It'll be a long drive, but probably we'll get there tomorrow really late or even in the wee hours of morning."

"Okay. Good. Your house is safe and dry here!"

"Thanks for taking care of it all for me, Joyce."

"It helped us both! Drive safe!"

After another glass of wine, Mia's mind turned like a filmstrip in reverse images of the months in Mexico. It went slow motion over the time with Jay—how they had parted friendly but detached, as if their laughter and easy conversations weren't unusual, as if the groove their bodies found wasn't worth further exploration or indulgence.

And then, her mind twisted back to winter.

"I can't think about you, Ger!" she sighed. "I'd think

it was all only a fantasy with you if I didn't have Peyton."

She sipped more wine.

"I didn't know I could love a man like you: a strong and quiet man with peaceful ways and hands that calmed me. I didn't know I could miss you so much, or learn how to breathe again without you here," she cried, and finished the bottle of wine.

Heartburn plagued her all night, and Peyton woke too early. Groggy, she pulled him into the bed and snuggled close until he went back to sleep. By the time he woke again, her head was pounding.

Peyton had oatmeal cooked in the microwave. Mia made coffee in a little coffee maker. They dressed and walked to the lobby. She fueled up with another cup of coffee and two sugary pastries.

As they drove north, Peyton played with his toys in the back seat. Mia turned on the radio to another oldies channel, and hit the freeway with a Chicago album playing, "Color My World."

Cars and trucks sped by. Her hands were shaky; her stomach was edgy, too.

They'd gone only nine miles when she saw a turnoff to a highway. "The direction we need to go: north, but through Central Oregon. Slower two-lane road to keep my sanity and safety. Hopefully," she said to herself. "Only seventy-one miles from Weed, California, to Klamath Falls, Oregon. I can make it *that* far."

The road climbed over hills with Mt. Shasta standing boldly in the rear-view mirror. Along the road, scrubby high elevation plants, rocks, pine trees and other evergreens dotted the landscape. There was little traffic. She drove fast.

"Isn't this fun, Peyton? Fifty miles to Oregon! Only a few more hours from there to the Columbia River and we'll be home!" But her face suddenly clouded with confusion. "We don't live on the Columbia. Gerald did."

She glanced into the mirror. "Listen to this story, Peyton. This is how you came to be! Important to know the beginning of your story. Places and people help make your life, but you add who you want to be. I didn't know that when I was little. I thought everything I was going to be was already set—maybe by family, God, fate. I didn't know there were many seeds growing a life. I didn't know I was deciding each step which seeds to scatter and water and grow new parts of myself. I didn't know my life had more possibility than one."

Smiling at him, she said "I met your daddy high above a river. A gust of wind blew me down, down into his arms. His place was a respite! But I left—left Portland, left

Tim, left Gerald and Oregon for Texas. Oh, Pey-Pey, the story is too complicated for you now! But one day, I'll tell you about losing Mother and finding Mama. That's how life is. When your heart breaks, it cracks open. Light and water seep in, bringing possibility to seeds buried and just waiting for essential nourishment."

Miles passed under the car wheels. A rest area beneath tall pines near Grass Lake Summit drew them over for a break from the car. They stretched their legs and had some snacks which held their appetites until Klamath Falls.

Mia stopped at a McDonalds on the north side of town. She ate a green salad while watching Peyton at the playground interacting with another toddler. They followed each other through the ball cage and up and over climbing equipment.

"That your boy?"

Mia turned to look into chocolate eyes on a face with stubbly beard. "Yes," she swallowed, looking back to the children running.

"How old?" he asked, taking in her face.

"Nineteen months."

"Mine, too. Toughies stick together," he laughed.

She smiled politely, began clearing her table.

"Don't go running off," the guy said suggestively.

Mia moved away, dumped the tray, retrieved her son, and left the premises. She drove slowly from the parking lot, eyes repeatedly checking behind for followers. "Geez! No one's tried to pick me up in a restaurant EVER! 'Forty-something' women with baby in tow is sexy? Really? Where's that going?"

Summer sun was shining down and the inside of the car had heated up. Wiping sweat from her neck, her fingers brushed against the smooth moonstone beads she'd put on in the motel last night.

Her eyes looked out at Klamath Lake. "See the water, Peyton? Isn't it pretty and blue? Maybe we'll see a pelican, or a crane. Maybe a bald eagle or osprey. Wouldn't that be awesome? Maybe we'll see them hunting: swooping down and catching a fish in their sharp talons."

He was watching the water, too, with expectant, dark eyes.

"So many things I will teach you, my son. Let's plan adventure vacations! What do you think of that? We'll make a map to record our outings. I wonder if there are travel writers writing 'Trips with Toddlers'?"

Mia laughed at the idea.

"It would have short chapters: activities interspersed with naps and feedings and diaper changes. Not to mention tips for clean-ups of vomit and spills! Maybe I'd feature the best products and procedures for every encountered complication. Maybe I'd become a more technical writer. How hard would it be?"

She quieted while driving through forests of tall pines, fir, and cedar. Aspen leaves fluttered on white branches.

"I like this. More space, less buildings and houses and streets and noise. Mexico has rubbed off on me. The slower pace of small towns is calming. You like this, too, don't you, Pey-Pey?"

His head was leaning against the side of the car seat and his eyes were closed.

She drove on, slowing only when going through hamlets of Crescent, Gilchrist, LaPine—timber towns now luring tourists and baby boomer generation retirees looking for outdoor lifestyles with golf, hunting, fishing, mountain and water sports enjoyed in over 300 days of sun per year.

When Peyton woke, he began fussing. She handed him various food items one at a time and he laughed at the game of grabbing them from her backward stretched hand and stuffing each fast in his mouth.

Watching for a convenient place to pull off to take a rest, Mia described the scenery as they went through Bend.

"There are lots of trees here, and a curving blue river cutting through the middle of town. Three tall pipes stand on a brick building. I'm not sure what those are; maybe smoke stacks from a factory or mill? A giant flag flies. The buildings are not as many or as big as Portland, or Seattle. It's a pretty town in the foothills of the Cascade Range. The mountains are mostly bare now. But I've seen pictures of winter: white snow dresses the peaks and makes a beautiful backdrop for sunrises and sunsets. Maybe we'll come back to the desert or high lakes when you're bigger. Maybe we'll camp. I've never done it, but we can learn together! Does it sound fun?"

Peyton threw bits of dry cereal across the car.

Eagle

Fifteen miles north of Bend, as they entered Redmond, Peyton let out a scream of frustration.

Turning a corner, she circled around a block to the main street, her eyes searching. "Yes!" Mia pulled to the curb beside an old brick building housing Herringbone Bookstore.

They went inside. Peyton ran down the roomy aisle to the children's section. Sample toys and books were on his level and he grabbed one after another.

"That's what they're for," a tall and youthful clerk standing behind the cash register said smiling.

"Thank you. We're a bit road weary."

"Can I help you find something?"

"No..." Mia's eyes scanned the long room with high ceilings. "This reminds me of a bookstore in The Dalles. Is there a 'recently published' section?"

"Something particular you want?"

"Yes, I'm a writer. My novel, *Mending Stone* has been out a few months. I'm just beginning marketing."

"We can order it. We also host author events in the store. Would you be interested in coming back to do a presentation about something related to your book?"

"Oh! Yes! I'd enjoy it very much."

"Leave me your contact information and we can set something up."

"Thank you."

Mia turned to see Peyton putting little plush sea creatures into a stuffed pelican's mouth and closing the bill, then taking them out of its stomach. "I told you we might see a pelican!"

The girl pointed to a high shelf holding boxed toys, including Hungry Pelican. "It has squeakers and rattles, different textures, and is great for cognitive and sensory development, fine motor skills."

"The bright colors are attractive and fun," Mia said.

"I'll buy one." While making the purchase, she remarked, "I could spend days looking through this store at everything offered! I'll be happy to return, and shop for more."

"Thank you," the clerk smiled. "See you again!"

Mia coaxed Peyton to the door. "Let's go see if we can feed the pelican something in our car."

They drove away. After another five miles, the highway entered a slow speed zone at a small community.

"What does Terrebonne mean? Is that French? 'Good earth'?" Mia mused at a sign.

A car ahead stopped suddenly as a pickup truck with hay bales hanging off the sides pulled slowly onto the highway. Mia braked hard.

"Geez! Crazy country drivers!" she yelled, glancing in the mirror at Peyton who was diligently trying to get out of his car seat straps. Looking up again, she saw a sign: green for a park/scenic area three miles to the east. She turned the wheel.

The road dipped down over rim rock into a green valley of farms and ranches. She passed a cemetery, turned at another sign, turned again and again, and drove up a lane to the parking area.

Peyton fussed and kicked and fought against the seat restraints as she was trying to release him.

"I know, darling. Me, too. I feel terrible. And the sun's so hot." She tried to put a hat and glasses on him, but he squirmed and grabbed them. "Okay, okay. We'll hang out in the shade under the junipers," she said pointing to a grassy area.

She lugged Peyton over to the payment box for park usage, and deposited the required fee. Sweating with effort, Mia carried him to a rustic restroom and stripped off his clothes and diaper, then doused him with water in the sink.

He laughed and splashed, soaking her.

"That feels great doesn't it?"

Mia splashed water to her face, slicked back her hair, doused her arms. She drenched his head. He shivered and laughed. She set him down naked on sandaled feet and he ran wild, slapping leather soles to the concrete floor. She glanced into the mirror, straightened her necklace, and was grabbing their things when the door opened.

He ran out.

Mia went after him.

Peyton ran headlong down a bumpy path through the trees and toward another trail coming up over the rim rock.

She dropped their things. "Peyton! Stop! Stop!"

But he was free and running.

"Peyton!" Her heart was pounding.

A man walking up over the rise just then grabbed Peyton, lifted and held the giggling and struggling boy.

Reaching them, Mia stretched out her arms to Peyton who leaned toward her with a grin. Tears sprang into her eyes.

The gangly man with grey whiskers and messy brown hair under a hat chuckled, "Got away from y' huh?"

She glanced up at him. "Yes. Getting so fast! Thank you so much!"

"No problem. My grandson goes naked wild every chance he gets," he laughed, wrinkles crinkling.

"I'm glad you were coming up right then."

"Be safe, but enjoy the outdoors," the man said, and went on his way toward the parking area.

Mia went with Peyton back toward the restroom.

A girl was picking the items she'd dropped and held them out to Mia.

"Thank you so much!"

"Sure," the girl said laughing at Peyton grinning at her. "Hi, kiddo!"

At a picnic table under the trees, Mia diapered and dressed him in shorts and a shirt, and managed to distract him with crackers long enough to get his hat with strap to stay on.

They ate and drank, and played tag running around and around the table. They drank sips of water from a squirt bottle. "Let's put our stuff away, then go explore," Mia suggested.

Back at the car, she grabbed Randi's generously sized scarf and used it to bind Peyton to her like some mothers do in Mexico with *rebozos*, traditional shawls worn by the countrywomen and used for a variety of purposes such as covering heads in bad weather, transporting goods, or wrapping and carrying babies.

Following the trail over the rim rock down switch backs, she worked their way down the steep hill. Several times her feet nearly slipped out on the dirt path, but she pushed on.

"Look down there, little man," she pointed. "See the Crooked River? Isn't it pretty? So blue cutting between walls of red rocks like a huge castle with a moat. You're a prince! And this is our place of magic. Already we've been blessed with assistance from a man and a girl: a knight and a princess!"

At the bottom of the hill, the trail crossed a wooden bridge and split into several paths: one following the river in each direction and another leading up and around the top of the tremendous rocks. Hikers were ahead on each of the trails, and climbers on ropes dangled from the cliffs.

"Oh, my gosh! Look at that," she gasped. "Eeekkk!" Mia shuddered. "Never do that! Never! Mama does not want you to be an extreme risk taker!"

Mia set Peyton down. He ran the wide and mostly level dirt trail with her close beside and able to grab him if he veered toward the river bank.

Ducks skimmed across the water.

A passing hiker pointed out an osprey nest topping a snag on the ridgeline across the narrow river. "I heard several bald eagles have been nesting nearby. I haven't seen them, though."

"I hope we do!"

"They're such spiritual beings," the guy observed.

She studied his brilliant blue hair, the synthetic, stretchy clothing he was wearing. "Do you rock climb?"

"Yeah. Come as often as I can. There are over a thousand climbs in this park. People travel from all over the world to try them. Most get hooked on the scenery and can't leave. This is pretty famous, even was featured in several movies and commercials, not just for the climbing, but because the rocks are so spectacular. You should see them at sunrise and sunset. Light bouncing off the stone makes them look as if lit from inside like gemstones."

Mia was nodding, studying him. "Is that all the gear you need to climb?"

"Ropes, shoes, belay devices, clamps, chalk, some pads to prevent scrapes."

"It seems so dangerous."

"Strenuous, but maybe not as dangerous as one might think with proper conditioning and strength, good equipment and partners. Lots of women do it! You should give it a try!"

She laughed, "Doubt I will. But who knows. Maybe someday when I'm back in shape!"

"Climb high like eagles! If you see one, it'll be a sign you should do it!" he winked.

"Right," she responded doubtfully.

"Start your little Running Eagle there early. Looks like a natural."

"Running Eagle?" Mia looked down at her son. Peyton was running in circles around them with his arms out like wings.

She walked further along the river before turning back. Climbers high up on the rocks in different spots and hikers at the top of the ridge looked down on them.

The sun was hot, but a late afternoon breeze started. They pushed on, crossing back over the bridge and up the steep hill, but the slippery sand and rocks were challenging for Peyton. Mia wrapped him tightly to her with the scarf again. It was slow going, and she was sweating and her legs were shaking from exertion when she reached the top.

Released finally from the tight binding, Peyton took off running. This time Mia let him go but was right behind making a game of snatching him up and letting him run again. He giggled so hard he could barely keep from stumbling. Finally, she hauled him to the car for a drink and a snack. He played with his toys. They hung out a few minutes, then went for a diaper change and cooled their hands and faces in the sink in the rest room.

Back in the car again, Mia said, "Well, Running Eagle, half-hour to Madras, only about two more hours to the Columbia. Nowhere closer we could stay except Shaniko, a little 'ghost town' on the road north toward Biggs, or maybe Maupin or Dufur on the road to The Dalles which is the shorter way home. Shall we wing it?"

But Peyton didn't make a noise, only stared straight ahead as if watching or waiting for something.

Mia ran her fingers over the moonstones still oddly cool on her neck. She sighed, and made a silent plea, "Please, Blessed Mother, direct our journey and choices along the way."

She started the engine and drove down the lane from the parking lot. Mia halted at a stop sign. She looked left, right, left again. Her foot ready to push the accelerator, paused. Her eyes were on a figure approaching along the road's shoulder. She studied the lean but muscular body, the bare legs and arms moving closer and closer. Blond hair was sticking out beneath a wide-brimmed khaki hat. Mia drew a sudden breath, and rolled down her window. "Smith Rock is crossed off my list of places to see."

Jay's face lit with surprise. He walked over to the car, glanced into the back seat at Peyton, then turned his smile to Mia.

"Amazing timing. I was here at dawn, worked all day. Got home and it was so hot in the house, thought I'd walk down by the river before supper for a change. Didn't get far before seeing a doe about to jump out into traffic. I ran at her and yelled and she veered off in the other direction. My adrenaline was pumping; I walked fast the rest of the way here."

She nodded, her fingers touching the moonstones at her neck. "Timing is everything. We made dozens of stops and starts with no plan except to drive north from San Francisco to Seattle. All to arrive here at just the right time to glimpse a familiar face I am truly surprised to see again."

"Where're you headed now?"

"We were just discussing the options of driving on and where to stay the night."

"I have a suggestion."

She smiled up at him. "Do you?"

"I live nearby. You could come over, have a bite to eat. We could catch up. If you want, stay over."

She smiled again. Unlocked the car doors.

Jay got in, and directed Mia to his house. "It's pretty basic," he said opening the front door. "But meets my needs. I'm not here much. In fact, I have to be in Bend early in the morning for a meeting. Might not even have time for my walk tomorrow."

She nodded, her eyes glancing around the small, hot room with little furniture, stacks of magazines piled on wood crates used for end tables, a rocking chair and straight back chair, an old oak dining table.

Jay opened the back door for a black Labrador to come inside.

"This is Dopey. He's a bit of a knuckle head."

The dog ran up and nosed Mia and nearly knocked over Peyton before she snapped up her boy.

"Dopey, come on," Jay grabbed the dog's collar and steered him away. "Want something to drink?" He went over to the refrigerator. "Looks like I need to do shopping. Try one of my concoctions." He extracted two bottled but label-less beers, cracked the tops off, and handed her one. "Maybe we can go up to Terrebonne Depot for something to eat in a while."

Mia nodded, "I noticed it on our way down from the highway," she said following him out back to a fenced area with spotty brown grass.

"I need to exercise the dog," Jay said picking up a ball thrower and sending a tennis ball sailing to the far corner of the yard. The dog took off like a bullet. "Dopey could do this all night! But I stop after about fifty throws."

"Wow," she nodded, watching Peyton toddling across a strip of rough concrete to a bucket of water. She lured him away by pulling a piece of rope found nearby.

"Sorry. Not baby proof. Things were a bit out of control this summer. The kids were here but busy in programs every day hiking, rock climbing, fishing, all the outdoor sports. Evenings we went swimming or to the arcade or movies to keep cool."

"Sounds like they're adventurous like you."

He smiled with pride, then wrenched the ball from Dopey's mouth, and threw it again. "We had a great time. Sometimes we stayed in Bend at my friend Kelli's house.

She works for me part-time since shortly after I returned from Mexico. She's cool."

"So…" Mia's brow furrowed. "Are the two of you dating?"

"We've been hanging out a lot," Jay said. "Nothing exclusive."

"Would she have a problem with me being here?"

"Probably not," he smiled. "I'd ask her to join us for a bite, but she's working in Bend."

Mia sipped the beer.

Jay kept throwing the ball.

"I enjoyed our time in Mexico," she said quietly.

"I did, too. How's the grief processing coming along?"

"Actually, I feel as if I'm getting closer to the life I want. I have a book signing coming up in The Dalles, and another in Seattle soon. I'm making some connections and have marketing and writing ideas; I can go at whatever pace I want. But the timing seems good. And I feel stronger, more capable."

He glanced over and grinned. "Just a few more throws."

She took sip of bitter ale and watched Peyton heading for the dirty bucket of water again. "Actually, I think we should be going. Just before turning to go to the park, I saw a grocery at the top of the hill. I need diapers for Peyton. Then I think we'll keep driving up to the Columbia."

"Sounds like a reasonable plan. Kids are a lot to handle on trips," Jay remarked stopping throwing the ball. Dopey went over and lapped up half the pail of water.

Mia carried Peyton back through the house and out to the car with Jay following. She strapped Peyton into his seat, and turned.

Jay's light blue eyes with golden flecks stared down at her. His hands gripped her shoulders. "Good seeing you."

"Amazing we arrived on the lane when we did…"

He kissed her forehead. "Magic happens every day."

She smiled at him, and breathed, "Thank you, Jay."

"Keep building your list of amazing things!"

"I will." She hugged him, then pulled away.

"Take good care of yourself and your little guy," he said as she got into the car and rolled down the window.

"I am. I truly am," Mia answered smiling back at him.

Jay tapped the car with his hand, and waved good-bye as she backed out.

Mia wiped sweat from her neck, and words were in her mind.

Only one

Other fill-ins

can't touch the place

where your hands

and words

and warming looks

reached me

Ohhh how that tap

struck me deep

And I did weep

But now I remember

you are here

in a breath of wind

on my neck

like cushioning lips

Epilogue

Mia drove north on Highway 97. At the junction of Highway 197, she veered toward The Dalles. The road wound over sage and juniper covered hills of dry grass.

"Peyton, isn't this exciting? We've never been here before! It's pretty. The spare vegetation reminds me of Mexico. I bet Nana Lia would like it, too! I met Daddy just north and a east of here. He loved this dry land."

"Dada! Dada!"

"Yes," Mia sighed. "Daddy loves you. I love you. We're a lucky family." She looked at him in the mirror. Her brow furrowed. Mia picked up her phone. When the call was done, she drew a shaky breath, and smiled.

Evening sun was shining. She rolled down the windows, and warm air rushed in. "Isn't this wonderful, Pey-Pey? I feel so alive!" Mia squealed.

They drove across the Deschutes River at Maupin, up and over the hill and down to Tygh Valley where lines of irrigation sprinklers shot water in swooshes onto green fields. "It's good to see things growing, isn't it, Peyton?"

Mt. Hood stood in the west. Most of its snow was gone now, and rocks jutted out. "How lovely you are in your white summer lace," she sighed. "You stand and watch and reach high. You don't worry who passes by. You don't worry what you will wear, what tomorrow will bring, how the seasons melt you down or build you up. You simply stand in splendor."

In the distance to the east, giant white wind turbines—sending shivers of dread through her several years ago—now slowly turned like clock hands.

They passed a little town and houses perched on hillsides surrounded by fields. Tall pines swayed in evening breezes and she could almost hear their whirring, whispering words like prayers.

Over the top of other rises were more fields, cherry orchards, and the Columbia River Gorge below.

"Peyton! We made it! There's The Dalles! That's where Daddy was born, where he went to school, where his grandmother, Charlotte, lived. She had the most beautiful garden." Mia drew a slow breath as if the scent of flowers was present.

She drove through downtown—past white towers of the old Sunshine mill and biscuit factory now made into a wine tasting venue, past the pioneer scene painted on the side of an old building, past Klindt's Booksellers where she would do her book signing. A brew pub with old clock tower prompted familiar words:

Time! Change come. Wake up!

Her eyes looked to St. Peters Landmark Church standing where it had been more than a hundred years. Its red bricks were glowing in the evening light and the rooster topping the spire pointed to the heavens.

A smile curved her lips.

Beyond motels and businesses and other attractions, she turned toward the Chenowith area outside The Dalles city limits. Down a short gravel road, she looked for the little house. Brown grass surrounded the crumbling sidewalk. Paint on the wood door had peeled and blown away.

Mia parked and unstrapped Peyton. They went up to the tidy house next door, and knocked. A barefoot woman with short curly grey hair opened the door.

"Hi, Dolores? I'm Mia. I called you? Gerald, my husband, was Charlotte's grandson. This is our son, Peyton."

"Hello!" the woman said smiling. "Just a minute." Leaving the door ajar, Dolores went into the house but returned a moment later wearing slip-on sandals. A key dangled on a string hanging from the pocket of her tropical print moo-moo. "Here we go."

They went over to Charlotte's house and used the key to open the front door. "I hope you don't mind," Dolores said, "I opened windows, washed up the linens and put them on the bed."

"It's fine. Perfect."

"I've been looking after the inside of the place since before Charlotte passed. She needed the help, and I was glad to do it. Gerald tried to pay me, but I refused while she was here with us. Since then, I didn't mind having a bit of spending money," the woman shrugged. She handed Mia the key.

"Thank you, Dolores, so much. You're an angel."

The woman waved away the comment with a flap of her hand, but smiled sweetly. "Nice to meet you both. I see the resemblance in the little guy. Good people: Charlotte and

Gerald. Good-night now."

Mia blinked back tears as Dolores went out.

Peyton was running through the house, back and forth, back and forth, making noise with his sandals on the bare floors.

Her eyes looked out the kitchen window to the yard, then she dialed her phone.

"Where are you?" Joyce asked.

"The Dalles."

"What do I hear? Footsteps? You sound grounded, too. Are you wearing the moonstones?"

"Yes," Mia laughed. "I was in a fog. But somehow, through a long series of stops and starts, we ran into a friend I'd met in Mexico."

"A *guy* friend?"

"I'll tell you all about it sometime. The connection with Jay *was* real, but there were no strings of expectation on us. It was good to see him again. *And* to release him."

"Uh, huh."

"As I was driving north across the high desert of Central Oregon, I felt something shifting. And when I drove toward The Dalles, suddenly the answer became clear!"

"What?"

"After Gerald passed, I discovered he owned Charlotte's house. It was tied up in Probate, but a few weeks ago I learned it was clear, and it's mine, with no debt."

"Oh, wow! If you sell this Seattle house, you'll be mortgage free. You can write to your heart's content. Or do anything you want!"

"That's what I'm thinking. It takes the financial pressure off. And there are roots here for Peyton."

Joyce sighed, "We'll be in separate states again."

"What's a little distance between friends?" Mia laughed. "I love you, Joyce."

"I love you, too, Sister."

After bathing Peyton, Mia rocked him in her arms, then put him to sleep on soft old linens folded and stacked on the floor beside Charlotte's bed. She brought their things in from the car, and closed the door. Beside it, the old framed photograph still hung on the wall—Charlotte holding a large baby with dark eyes and hair.

"Watch over us," Mia whispered.

Wandering to the back yard, she sat down on the bench in the garden. Her eyes searched beyond the weeds to see how it had been three years ago—white alyssum blooming in thick tufts, delicate blue delphiniums and red bleeding hearts hanging like ornaments from slender branches, white lilies trumpeting blasts of gold, a leggy, purple clematis twining around a rough ladder leaning against the weathered cedar fence, pink roses with spots of red achingly beautiful. "This is just heavenly!" Mia had gushed. "It must be a lot of work!"

"Good gittin' hands in dirt. Y' could use some earth on y'," Charlotte had replied as Mia looked down at tiny blue flowers on dense green foliage surrounding a birdbath.

"Forget-Me-Nots," Gerald had said.

"I won't forget you," she now whispered, her eyes glancing to a bright star with the moon hanging beside it like a crooked smile.

"I won't forget you either, Charlotte," Mia chuckled. "You asked me long ago if I was glad I came." Tears sprang to her eyes. "Yes. So glad for every moment. Thank you for growing a kind man. I'll work hard to grow another good man."

The sky had turned from blue to brilliant red. More stars were appearing: twinkling lights seeding hope.

Tomorrow's plans could wait.

Mia leaned down and pulled a few weeds at her feet. She pulled a few more, and a few more, working into the late hours with the moon and stars lighting her way.

~~~

Attractions

San Bartolome Quialana

Oaxaca, Mexico

Hierve el Agua

80 KM from Oaxaca City

Off Hwy 179

www.visitmexico.com

Playas Zicatela & Carrizalillo

Puerto Escondido, Oaxaca, Mexico

Sky Harbor International Airport

3400 E. Sky Harbor Blvd.

Phoenix, Arizona 1-602-273-3300

skyharbor.com

Grand Canyon National Park

www.nps.gov/grca

Golden Gardens Park

8498 Seaview PL NW

Seattle, WA 98117

206-684-4075

www.seattlegov/parks/park

Adams Elementary

6110 28th Avenue NW

Seattle, Washington 98107

1-206-252-1300

adam,es.seattleschools.org

TM Dessert Works

6116 Phinney Avenue N

Phinney, WA 98103

206-789-5765

tmdessertworks.com

Kens Market

7231 Greenwood Ave N

Seattle, WA 98103

206-784-3470

www.kensmarket.com

St. James Cathedral

804 9th Avenue

Seattle, Washington 98104

www.stjames-cathedral.org

Seattle-Tacoma Airport—WA

www.portseattle.org/sea-tac

Seattle Children's Hospital
4800 Sand Point Way NE
Seattle, Washington 98105
206 987-2000

Dave Mackie Park
7490 Maxwelton Road
Clinton, Washington
http://www.portofsouthwhidbey.com

Seattle Children's Museum
305 Harrison Street
Seattle, Washington 98109
1-206-441-1768
www.thechildrensmuseum.org

Neil's Clover Patch Café
14485 WA-525 #3
Langley, Washington 98260
1-360-321-4120

Washington Park Arboretum
2300 Arboretum Drive East
Seattle, Washington 98112
1-206-543-8800
www.depts.washington.edu

Langley Chamber of Commerce
208 Anthes Avenue
Langley, WA 98260
360-221-6765
www.visitlangley.com

Seattle Japanese Garden
1075 Lake Washington Blvd. E.
Seattle, Washington 98112
1-206-684-4725
www.seattlejapanesegarden.org

Saratoga Inn
201 Cascade Avenue
Langley, Washington 98260
1-360-221-5801
saratogainnwhidbeyisland.com

Mukilteo Ferry
Mukilteo, WA 98204
www.wsdot.wa.gov./ferries

Langley Clock & Gallery
Down the Lane at 220 2nd Street
Langley, WA 98260
360-221-3422

The Resort at Skamania Coves

45932 WA-14

Stevenson, Washington 98648

1-509-427-4900

www.skamaniacoves.com

The Dalles Bridge, Lock & Dam

US Army Corps of Engineers

541-506-7819

www.nwp.usace.army.mil/locations

Celilo Village

I-84 Columbia River E. of The Dalles

Sam Hill Memorial Bridge

US 97 & I-84 Biggs Junction

Columbia River near Maryhill

Klindt's Booksellers

315 East 2nd Street

The Dalles, OR 97058

541-296-3355

www.klindtsbooks.com

Multnomah Falls Lodge

50000 E. Historic Columbia R. Hwy

503-695-2376

www.multnomahfallslodge.com

La Traviata

314 Congress Avenue

Austin, Texas 78701

1-512-479-8131

www.latraviatatx.com

La Olita

Las Brisas de Zicatells, Oaxaca

+52 984 119 6139

Puerto Escondido, Oaxaca

El Cafecito

Boulevard Benito Juarez 1,

Seccion C, Local 01, Rinconada

71983 Puerto Escondido, Oaxaca

+52 954 582 3465

Hotel Don Cenobio

Av Juarez No. 3 Centro

San Pablo Villa de Mitla

Mitla, Oaxaca, 70430 Mexico

1-800-491-6126

www.hoteldoncenobio.com

Voodoo Donuts

22 SW 3rd. Street

Portland, OR 97204

1-241-4704

www.voodoodonut.com

Dry Creek Inn, Best Western

198 Dry Creek Road

Healdsburg, California 95448

707-433-0300

www.drycreekinn.com

Lykke Li

www.lykkeli.com

San Francisco Zoo

San Francisco, CA 94132

415-753-9080

www.sfzoo.org

Quarryhill Botanical Garden

12841 Hwy 12

Glen Ellen, CA 95442

707-996-3166

quarryhillbg.org

San Francisco International Airport

650-821-8211

www.flysfo.com

Maryhill Winery

9774 Lewis and Clark Highway 14

Goldendale, WA 98620

1-509-773-1976

www.maryhillwinery.com

Calistoga Parks and Recreation

1232 Washington Street

Calistoga, CA

1-707-942-2838

www.ci.calistoga.ca.us

Olive Pit

2156 Solano Street

Corning, CA 96021

1-530-824-4668

www.olivepit.com

Sisterhood of the Sacred Scarves

www.thespiritedwoman.com

Swiss Holiday Lodge

2400 S Mt. Shasta Blvd.

Mt. Shasta, CA 96067

1-530-926-3446

www.swissholiday.com

Gemstone Alchemy

703-763-1655

www.gemstonealchemy.com

The Crystal Room

109 W. Castle

Mt. Shasta, CA 96067

1-530-918-9108

www.crystalsmtshasta.com

Wayside Grill

2217 S. Mt. Shasta Blvd.

Mt. Shasta, CA 96067

1-530-918-9234

www.waysidegrill.com

McDonalds

Klamath Falls, OR 97601

541-882-9410

Bend Old Mill District

450 SW Powerhouse Dr. #422

Bend, OR 97702

1-541-312-0131

www.theoldmill.com

Herringbone Bookstore

422 SW 6th

Redmond, OR 97756

541-526-1491

www.herringbonebooks.com

Smith Rock State Park

Terrebonne, OR 97760

1-800-551-6949

http://oregonstateparks.org

Terrebonne Depot Food & Drink

400 NW Smith Rock Way

Terrebonne, OR 97760

1-541-548-5030

www.terrebonnedepot.com

Accuracy of information is attempted,
not guaranteed

Discussion Questions

1. What was most interesting about this story?

2. Could you envision the various settings?

3. What changes surprised you?

4. How do landscapes contribute to the story?

5. How do spiritual beliefs affect the characters?

6. If you have not read previous books in the *Possibility Series*, were you able to follow the story? Do you now want to read *Mending Stone* and *Catching Rain?*

7. Would you enjoy reading more books with these same characters, settings, or themes?

About the Author

Sharon Duerst was raised on the Columbia River Gorge. A graduate of University of Oregon, she has worked in a variety of settings: education, long term care, retail, and office. She enjoys many creative hobbies, and outdoor activities: walking, camping, and gardening.

Follow Sharon Duerst, Author

On Goodreads, Facebook, Twitter, Pinterest

Follow other writing and information at
www.mendingstone.com

www.ingramcontent.com/pod-product-compliance
Lightning Source LLC
Chambersburg PA
CBHW060401260626
47160CB00006B/2391